ONCE UPON A POWER PLAY

A RISKY BUSINESS NOVEL

JENNIFER BONDS

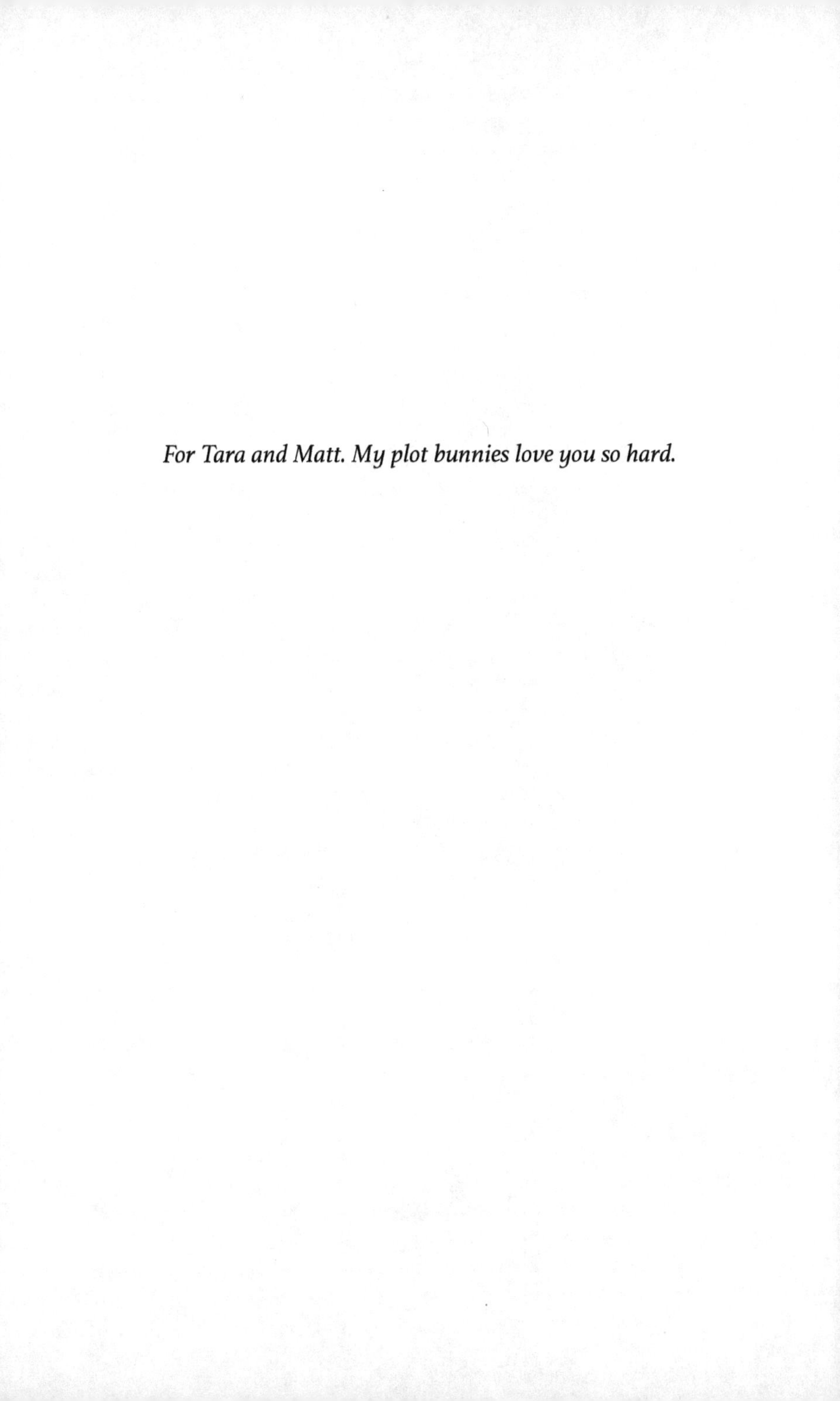

For Tara and Matt. My plot bunnies love you so hard.

1

CHLOE

Chloe Jacobs glared at her glowing cell phone, willing it to spontaneously combust in a raging ball of fire. The bigger, the better. She didn't care if the damn thing melted into a messy lump of plastic and metal right there on the coffee table.

It sure as hell beat the alternative: accepting that she had been dumped—*yet again*—by text.

What. The. Fuck.

Pretty classy of Dave to text her twenty minutes *after* he was supposed to pick her up.

Who *did* that? Oh, that's right. The losers she seemed to attract in droves.

And she fell for them every time. She'd even given Dave the benefit of the doubt, assuming the blizzard outside was to blame for his lateness.

Sucker.

There was no denying it. She had a weakness for underdogs, douchey pickup lines, and controlling, narcissistic jackasses who thought it perfectly acceptable to treat her like an accessory. A very temporary accessory.

That weakness was forever biting her in the ass.

Chloe sighed. She ran her hands over the fitted Tadashi sheath dress she'd splurged on for her date. The warm gold tones of the dress were the perfect complement to her dark hair and eyes, but the thing she loved most were the bands that crisscrossed her middle. Those little darlings gave her an honest-to-God hourglass figure. Not exactly an easy feat on a top-heavy shorty who topped out at five-foot three on a good day.

Hell, she'd even spent an hour wrestling her wild mass of curls into a fancy twist in an attempt to, what? Be more conservative? Polished? That's what Dave had wanted, wasn't it?

So much for that.

All dressed up and no place to go. It was starting to feel like the story of her life.

Well, *screw* Dave.

If she was going to spend Friday night holed up in her apartment wearing the nicest freaking dress she owned, she was going to do it with a margarita in her hand and a smile on her face. Which meant a trip to the bodega to grab a bottle of lime juice and maybe a pint of ice cream, snow be damned.

Grabbing her boots off the radiator, she was pleasantly surprised to find them warm and toasty when she shoved her feet into the furry lining.

Finally, something was going her way.

She slipped into her coat and tied the belt snug around her waist, knowing it would do little to ward off the biting wind that howled outside. But if that was the price of a good margarita, she'd pay it tonight. The only other option—wallowing in self-pity and wondering what was so wrong with her that she couldn't keep a man—wasn't exactly enticing.

Tucking her chin into the collar of her wool coat, she made the trek down the block to the little shop where she bought all her groceries. Not that she ever needed much since she was far from being a stellar cook. Which was, of course, on her mother's long list of reasons why she'd never land a decent man.

Like knowing how to braise a side of beef would make her more desirable to the opposite sex. Then again, maybe it would.

Hell if she knew what men wanted, aside from the obvious.

Another lonely Friday night was testament to that fact.

Although, technically, Dave hadn't really dumped her, had he?

It wasn't like they had a commitment. They'd only gone out a couple of times.

Sure, she was pissed he'd stood her up and blown her off via text, but even more so, she was angry at herself for giving him the opportunity.

Shivering, she pulled her coat tighter, wishing she'd grabbed a hat.

The sad truth was, she had *terrible* taste in men. Clearly her instincts were broken. Because if there was a creep within an eight-block radius, she'd probably dated him.

Yes, there were lots of eligible males in New York, but that didn't make them men. It just made them horny.

She'd been riding the loser train as long as she could remember, and she still wouldn't know a decent man if she tripped over him and landed on his disco stick.

Fucking Cinderella. This was all her fault.

Teaching little girls they should sit around and wait for Prince Charming to sweep them off their glass-slippered feet. Probably where she got her shoe fetish, too.

Well, she'd kissed her fair share of frogs, and there hadn't been a single prince in the bunch. Athletes, stockbrokers, starving artists... As far as she could tell, they were all cut from the same self-centered cloth.

Correction.

Athletes were the worst of the lot. Her college boyfriend, Shane the Speedo, the last of a long line of athletes she'd dated, had proven it when he dumped her for a leggy blond Tri Delt three weeks before graduation.

Stupid asshole.

He'd actually had the audacity to claim the Stepford replacement would be better for his image. His *image!* As if Chloe was nothing more than a starter girlfriend, bought and paid off with a fancy dinner that she'd expected to end with a proposal. She hadn't even sensed his betrayal coming.

Just thinking about it had her seeing red.

Which was exactly why she'd sworn off jocks.

Hell, she didn't even want to date a guy who went to the gym more than three days a week.

Chloe sighed, a frosty puff of air escaping her lips.

Perhaps it was time to focus some of that wasted energy on more productive endeavors, like her career. She'd been a Junior Associate at PBA for three painstaking years, and with her best friend Olivia leaving the company, things just weren't the same. There had been a lot of changes, not the least of which was her stepping up and taking on more challenging projects, which allowed her to showcase her social media expertise.

It seemed to be paying off, and people were starting to take notice.

At the ripe old age of twenty-five, she was finally a full-fledged adult. Maybe it was time to start acting like one and spend more time planning for her future and less time chasing a fairytale that hadn't quite materialized.

It was official. She was banning men indefinitely.

Shoes? Not so much.

Shit! A gust of wind whipped at her back and she lost her balance, nearly eating cement on the slick sidewalk in front of the store.

Grabbing a bike rack for leverage, she righted herself and shuffled toward the door.

What had she been thinking, traipsing down here in a cocktail dress?

She was *so* not dressed for the weather, but it was too late to turn back.

Brushing the wet snow from her hair and face, she opened the door and stepped inside.

Thankfully, the store was much warmer.

She waved to the girl behind the counter and stomped her boots on the soggy rug. Bypassing the shopping baskets, she headed straight to the freezers and grabbed a pint of dark chocolate toasted coconut ice cream. If that didn't take the sting off her craptastic evening, a stiff drink would surely do the trick.

She made a beeline for the lime juice, only to be met with an empty shelf.

Damn.

Disappointment washed over her. Mixers were the devil, but she grabbed a bottle of the greenish yellow belly-wash anyway.

Silently, she prayed the store had fresh limes. She wasn't above squeezing them herself, but the produce selection usually left something to be desired.

Slipping between a rack of potato chips and a display of cereal, she took a shortcut into the next aisle, which held a couple of small coolers and a limited selection of fresh fruits and vegetables. Her eyes swept over the display.

Jackpot!

There was one lonely green fruit sitting in the basket, screaming *Margarita, baby!* Just as she reached for it, someone snatched the lime out of her grasp.

2

RYAN

SCORE! Ryan Douglas grabbed the last lime, thankful the tiny store had at least one item he needed in stock. He shook his head. Back home, people didn't go crazy and clean out the grocery store every time it snowed. As far as he could tell, east coasters labored under the delusion they'd be snow bound for days every time a flake dropped from the sky.

It was the craziest damn thing he'd ever seen, and after five years in the city, he still didn't get it.

"Hey! That's mine!"

He froze in his tracks, slowly turning around to find a tiny, pissed off brunette glaring at him with one hand on her hip and the other hugging a gallon-sized jug of margarita mix. "Excuse me?"

"The lime," she said, nodding her head and enunciating each word as if he might not speak English. "I saw it first."

It was impossible to suppress the grin that spread over his face. Was she serious?

His gaze raked over her, taking in the fancy upsweep of her dark hair and the lacy gold dress—if you could call it that—that revealed more than it covered peeking out from under her unbuttoned coat. The furry brown boots climbing halfway to her bare knees? Those he could do without, but the rest was pretty damn sexy. There wasn't a winter coat around that could hide those curves. She had the kind of body a man could sink his teeth into. And he. Was. Ravenous.

"Like what you see?" She raised her brow and hooked a thumb over her shoulder. "The meat department is two aisles over."

He laughed, and it was an honest-to-God, full-on belly laugh. She was a fiery little thing.

That didn't mean he was giving her the lime.

Maybe if she'd asked nicely. But with that attitude? It'd be a cold day in hell.

"Last I heard, possession is nine-tenths of the law." He tossed the lime in the air and caught it with his right hand.

She glared at him, and for a moment he thought she'd kick him in the balls with her big furry boots. He was being an ass, but she wasn't exactly Miss Manners herself. Besides, it was the most fun he'd had all day. Which spoke volumes about his shitty afternoon, most of which had been spent getting his ass kicked by a sadistic physical therapist. His leg hurt like hell, but he'd tough it out.

He had no other choice if he wanted to salvage his career.

The brunette rolled her eyes, the dark irises shimmering like black coffee under the soft glow of the overhead lights. "It's not my fault you have inhumanly long lumberjack arms."

The smirk that followed told him yes, she was in fact referring to his worn flannel shirt.

Typical self-important New York princess, judging him by something so superficial.

Not that he gave a fuck what she thought, but man, what he wouldn't give to wipe that little grin off her heart-shaped face. And with years of experience antagonizing his two older sisters, he had a pretty good idea of how to do it. He waved the lime in front of her again, wondering if she'd try to make a play for it. Not that she could get her hands on it if he didn't want her to. He towered over her by nearly a foot, and his reflexes were pretty damn good.

"Princess, I wouldn't give you this lime if you got down on your knees and begged, but if it means that much to you, you're welcome to give it a go."

Her jaw dropped. And the zing of pleasure he got at seeing her speechless? That felt pretty damn good.

Truth was, he could live without the lime, but he wasn't about to hand over his fruit to a pushy, sarcastic, smart-mouthed, little spitfire. Even if she did have the kind of curves that could bring a man to his knees.

Hell, especially then. He'd been down that road before and all it brought was trouble.

The truth was, although they shared zero physical characteristics, her attitude reminded him of Kelsey, the woman who'd abandoned him in his darkest hour and shredded his heart without a second thought. He didn't need Freud to figure out why he was getting such a thrill out of goading the sexy stranger. Displaced anger and all that psychobabble bullshit.

"Nice boots, by the way."

Blood rushed to her cheeks, coloring them a deep crimson. She sputtered, her gaze dropping to her feet before slamming back into him with confidence. "What? You want to see if they come in your size?"

"Is that what you're into?" A smirk tugged at the corner of his mouth. She had a quick wit, but as the youngest of six kids, he'd learned long ago not to be anyone's punching bag. "Kinky, princess. Hate to break it to you, but I wouldn't be caught dead wearing anything that looked like it had been skinned from a Wookiee."

She scrunched up her pert little nose and for the first time he noticed the dusting of freckles on her cheeks. "Listen, Paul Bunyan, I don't know what the hell a Wookiee is, but—"

"Wait. What?" He groaned and scrubbed a hand over his face. "You're kidding, right? Chewbacca?"

She threw up her hands, looking as confused as he felt.

"Star Wars?" he asked, hard pressed to believe he'd wasted such a good comeback on the one person on the planet who'd never watched the movies. "Seriously. You've never seen it?"

"Yeah, no." She rolled her eyes again and crossed her arms over her chest, giving her breasts a very distracting and wholly unnecessary boost. "Do I look like a Trekkie to you?"

He snorted. No, she most certainly did not look like any Trekkie he'd ever seen, which explained the sudden interest his cock had taken in their little sparring match. Apparently his brain wasn't the only part of him envisioning more productive uses for those pouty little lips of hers. If she needed a lesson, he'd be more than happy to give it to her, but he had something a little darker in mind. "You do know that's a totally different movie franchise, right?"

She wrinkled her brow. "Star Wars, Star Trek? What the hell is the diff—"

"Open up that register and put your hands in the air! Now!"

Fuuuuck.

3

___

CHLOE

"You've got to be kidding me," Chloe muttered, refusing to believe her ears, or her eyes. Twenty-five years of living in the city and she'd never once been touched by its violence. Never been scammed, or mugged, or even had her goddamn pocket picked. There was no way she'd stumbled into an armed robbery.

No. Way.

But, yeah, it was definitely happening. Right now. In the bodega.

The proof stood fifty feet away—give or take—wielding a gun and looking cracked out of his ever-loving mind.

Fear blossomed in her belly, a tremor crawling up her spine and taking root.

When Lumberjack Boy clamped a hand over her mouth and pulled her behind a tower of Cheerios, crushing her to his solid chest and shielding her with his mammoth body, her fears were reaffirmed. With her brain on high alert, she couldn't help but notice the masculine scent of soap and spice that clung to his body. Or that the hands wrapped around her were both soft and strong, scooping her up and holding her secure, as though she weighed nothing at all.

When he gently set her back on the floor, she pulled away from him immediately, putting as much distance between their bodies as the small space allowed.

It wasn't much considering he was a freaking giant.

Out of sight, they crouched together and watched the scene at the front of the store unfold, helpless to stop it.

"I said open up that register and give me the cash, bitch!" the robber yelled, waving his pistol around like Annie Oakley.

Her stomach dropped. Dude was totally unstable.

"I think I'm gonna pee my pants."

Lumberjack Boy's head whipped around, full lips pressed in a grim line.

Oops. She hadn't meant to say that out loud.

His eyes darted to her stocking covered legs and something wicked flared in his eyes, sending a heat wave to her center. "You're not wearing any pants, princess."

She nearly laughed at the absurdity of his observation, and her body's reaction to him. Only that was likely to get them discovered and quite possibly shot, judging by the ranting of the nut job up front.

Forcing herself to table her misplaced arousal, she peeked around the corner.

"Bitch, you better open that register if you know what's good for you!" the guy yelled.

The cashier was crying, trying to explain through her tears she couldn't open the register without completing a transaction. Even from a distance, Chloe could see her hands shaking.

What would he do if the girl couldn't get him cash?

She didn't want to find out.

Apparently Paul Bunyan was thinking the same thing. "We can't just sit here. We have to do something."

"Yeah, call the police," she whispered, resting her chin on

her knees and sucking in a deep breath. She did not want to die in a damn grocery store. Wearing her best dress, nonetheless.

He studied her with blue eyes so clear and bright they reminded her of the summer sky—something she hoped to see again if they survived this little adventure. "The police may not get here in time. I'm going in for a closer look."

"Have you lost your mind?" She squeaked, hating the way her words were laced with terror. Since they were two aisles past the register and hidden from view, the guy had no idea they were even in the store. Surely that was a good thing. God only knew what he'd do if they spooked him. "He has a gun!"

"Look." He gestured to the front of the store, ridiculously calm given they were living out their very own, very terrifying episode of *Law & Order*. "It's just some punk kid, but if he does something to that girl, I'll never forgive myself."

"Some punk kid who's packing heat and probably high as a kite!"

His lips twitched. The cocky bastard. "All the more reason not to wait for the cops. He doesn't even know we're here, which gives me an advantage. Besides, he's probably scared, just like us. Stay here and call the police. I'm going up there."

Scared like us? Because the lumberjack sure as hell didn't seem afraid in the least.

No, he surveyed the store with a deep-seated calm that was hard for her panic-stricken brain to comprehend, his eyes sweeping over the cashier, the robber, and the aisles that separated them. Was he playing out the scene in his mind, planning his next move?

Curious about the lime-stealing jerk who seemed so immune to fear, she studied his profile. Despite his obnoxious disposition, he wasn't terrible to look at. Her eyes dropped to his ass, finding it firm, round, and swathed in denim that fit like a second skin over his muscular butt and thighs.

Okay, fine. Flannel shirt or not, the man was hot. Drool worthy, even.

With a backward ball cap pinning his shaggy brown hair back, she had a clear view of his face. Strong jaw, slightly crooked nose, intense eyes. *Really* intense eyes. The kind that could overpower a woman, making her forget her resolve.

Good thing he wasn't her type.

At. All.

Besides, she was swearing off men.

She gave herself a mental shake. Now was hardly the time to dwell on her disastrous love life.

When her human shield crept down the aisle, crouching on his haunches, she grabbed his shirt, cursing herself for noticing the well-defined muscles of his back and shoulders. "Be careful."

After all, she didn't want the big dumb oaf to get shot playing hero.

He glanced over his shoulder and smiled, his eyes crinkling in the corners. "Look at the bright side. Dead men don't need limes."

Glaring at him for all she was worth, she crept along behind him, fishing through her bag in search of her phone.

4

RYAN

R YAN INCHED DOWN THE AISLE, cursing his bad luck and the pain shooting through his right calf. It was like being stabbed with a hot poker over and over. Blowing out a calming breath, he pushed the pain aside and focused on the girl behind the register. She was scared shitless. And who could blame her?

The kid was screaming obscenities in her face.

When he reached over the counter and grabbed the front of her shirt, Ryan's gut clenched.

He'd have to act fast. The situation was spiraling out of control and there was no way he was going to cower in the shadows, leaving the girl utterly defenseless. God forbid his sisters were ever in this situation, but if they were, he hoped someone would do the same for them, stranger or not.

In an attempt to hide his face from security cameras, the robber had pulled up the hood of his jacket. That was good news at least. While it obscured his face, it had to be blocking his peripheral vision, too. If he was quick, Ryan could probably take the kid down before he knew what hit him.

He braced himself to lunge, knowing the action would be hell on his injured leg.

Ready.

Set.

Crash!

He whipped around. The woman in the gold dress stared at him, frozen in fear, dark eyes wide. A can of peas rolled across the floor, stopping only when it met the toe of his boot.

What the hell did she think she was doing? She was going to get herself killed, along with everyone else in the store.

What part of "stay put and call the cops" hadn't she understood?

"Who's there?"

Fuck. So much for the element of surprise.

"Get on out here before I put a bullet in this girl's face!"

The cashier screamed, her terror echoing through the small store and penetrating right down to his bones.

"Stay back and stay hidden," he whispered, cupping the chin of his less than stealthy companion and forcing her to focus on his eyes. "I'm going to take care of this, but whatever happens, you stay out of sight. I'll keep you safe. Understand?"

She swallowed and nodded, her chin quivering.

Her fear called to him, demanding he keep his promise. The look in her eyes, the tremble of her lips—they tapped into the protective, archaic, caveman side of him that would do anything for a woman in distress.

He just hoped he wouldn't let her down.

Putting his hands in the air, he slowly stepped into the open, careful not to make any sudden moves that would alarm the trigger-happy robber.

"Who the fuck are you?" The kid stepped back, flicking his gun toward the cashier and motioning Ryan to join her so he could keep them both in his line of sight.

"Look, man, I'm nobody. Just stopped in to pick up a few things before the snow shuts the city down." He moved toward the girl, using the opportunity to inch within arm's reach of his target. Had he lost his mind? It was starting to feel like a suicide mission, but he had to stick to the plan, if only to protect the women. Who the hell knew if the cops were even on the way? And if they were, the weather outside would undoubtedly delay them. Talk about a perfect storm. He needed to get this situation unfucked—*now.* "I don't want any trouble. I'll tell you what, she can swipe my card to open the register. Everybody wins, nobody gets hurt."

The kid thought it over, his eyes moving frantically between Ryan and the cashier.

Yep. Definitely high. Or tweaking, which was probably a good thing.

Otherwise he'd realize Ryan's offer was bullshit. The cashier didn't need a card to open the register.

The kid sniffed and wiped his nose. Finally, he nodded. "No funny business."

Reaching into his back pocket, he pulled out his wallet. He held it high in the air, doing his best to look unthreatening and compliant.

When the tweaker shifted his attention to the cashier again, he made his move.

Shooting forward, he grabbed the kid's wrists and forced the gun into the air. Underweight and in need of a good meal, he didn't stand a chance. Their bodies spun around as they grappled for control of the gun. Ryan brought his knee up, burying it in the guy's stomach. Just as he was about to take him down, a flash of gold caught the corner of his eye.

One loud *thunk* later, the tweaker dropped face down on the floor.

Holy. Shit.

The little vixen stood over his limp body, a look of surprise etched on her face.

She'd clocked him with her purse. Her fucking *purse.*

He hadn't noticed before, but the thing was a monster. Probably weighed half as much as she did, judging by the size. Unable to believe his eyes, he nudged the kid with his boot. "He's out cold."

She smiled up at him triumphantly, not a hair out of place. "Should I hit him with pepper spray, too?"

Incredulous, he stared at her, unable to form words.

Well, at least not any with more than four letters.

Drawing a deep breath, he pulled his hat off and pushed his hair back before repositioning the cap on his head. Who was this chick?

"Talk about an adrenaline rush." She kneeled down to investigate her handiwork, completely oblivious to his horror.

"What the hell were you thinking?" he asked, not bothering to mask his irritation. While he totally supported women's rights, he didn't quite think it should extend to impeding a robbery or attacking a gun toting speed freak. "I told you to call the police!"

Planting a hand on her hip, she rose to her full height and lifted her chin.

He wasn't sure what kind of men she was used to dealing with, but if she seriously thought he was going to crack in the face of five and a half feet of hotness wrapped in gold lace, she had another think coming.

"What was *I* thinking?" she asked. "First of all, I'm not the one who decided to jump the gun wielding meth head! Second of all, you are not the boss of me."

He snorted. Thank God for small favors.

It would take a strong man to handle all that sass on a daily basis. Or a masochist.

"I'm not the boss of you? Is that all you've got, princess, or is there a legitimate reason you didn't call for help?"

She muttered something under her breath that sounded an awful lot like *jackass*. "I would have called if I'd had my phone."

"Really? That big ass purse of yours can take a man down, but you're telling me there's no phone in there?" he asked, the inexplicable need to stoke the fire rising once again. "Just my luck. Stuck in an armed robbery with the only woman in New York who doesn't carry a phone in her purse."

She shrugged, not looking apologetic in the least. "I was mad at my phone so I left it at home."

Un-fucking-believable. He pinched the bridge of his nose. "And that didn't seem worth mentioning at the time?"

"I forgot."

"You know what? Never mind."

Bending down, he picked up the gun and tucked it in the waistband of his jeans before approaching the check stand

The girl behind the register watched their exchange with interest.

"Are you okay?" Offering what he hoped was a reassuring smile, he placed a tentative hand on her shoulder. She nodded absently, her eyes flitting to his face. Recognition dawned. "You should probably call 911. She really walloped him, but he won't be out long."

Leaning a hip into the counter, he watched as she punched 9-1-1 into the phone and relayed the events of the last ten minutes to the emergency responder.

Had it only been ten minutes? It felt like a lifetime.

So much for a quiet Friday night.

He eyed the brunette, who was doing her best to ignore him, focusing her attention everywhere but his direction. A smirk played on his lips. "So what the hell is in that bag anyway?"

Her head swiveled in his direction, and she arched her brow. She was pissed off and it was sexy as hell. "Oh, now you approve?"

He threw his head back and laughed. "I'm Ryan, by the way."

5

———

CHLOE

"ARE YOU EVEN LISTENING TO ME?" Chloe asked, hurling a whole lot of sarcasm at the distracted cop who was supposed to be taking her statement. Perhaps if New York's finest could tear his attention away from Paul Bunyan's ungrateful twin for two seconds, he'd be able to wrap up her statement and save her the trouble of repeating the story for a third time. Much as she enjoyed reliving the thrill of dropping that thug like a stone, she wanted to go home and drown herself in a margarita already.

She sure as hell deserved it after the night she'd had.

To add insult to injury, the cops had literally flipped a coin to see which of them would take her statement. *A coin!* Like it was going to be so God-awfully bad to get stuck with her.

What was up with that?

She cut her eyes at Ryan. What the hell was he telling the police officer anyway?

The guy was hanging on his every word. So was the cashier. As if he'd been the one to save her ass.

Not that she expected undying gratitude, but a simple thanks would have been nice.

When Ryan started wrestling that kid for the gun, she'd

seriously thought she might faint. But no, instinct had taken over, driving her into the fray when common sense told her to run the other direction. Not that she'd had much choice. Knowing there was no help coming, she couldn't very well stand there and do nothing while he risked his life to save them.

Even if he was the world's biggest jackass.

When the cop finally cut her loose, she purchased her margarita mix, deciding to forgo the ice cream, which had long since melted. Before she could make her escape, Ryan intercepted her, blocking the exit with his supersize self.

"You never gave me your name." He flashed her a thousand-watt smile, complete with perfect white teeth and an adorable little dimple.

It might have melted her panties any other day. Any day except this one.

She was done with men. Especially the slick, confident, jerky ones who never stuck around and trampled her heart on the way out the door.

"Yeah, that was intentional." She tied the belt on her coat, doing her best to appear calm and in control despite the adrenaline cranking through her veins. Probably why her stupid heart skipped a beat, too. It sure as hell wasn't that smile. Or the way his long hair brushed his shoulders, an unspoken warning: *bad boy at play.* "Excuse me."

"Suit yourself." He dropped his arm so she could squeeze past. A gust of wind slapped her in the face when she stepped outside. Figured. The snow hadn't let up and if anything, it was colder and windier than it had been an hour ago. "But I'd prefer to know the name of the woman I'm walking home."

She stopped dead in her tracks, ignoring the snow that billowed around them.

"Wrong answer." Hoping to drive her point home, she poked him in his big stupid chest for good measure.

"It wasn't a question." He jammed his hands in the pockets of his jeans, looking up and down the street. Apparently all the sane people had already taken refuge indoors. "No way am I going to let you go traipsing around alone in this storm. It's not safe."

"It's fine," she argued, waving her hand dismissively. The odds of being victimized twice in one night were pretty slim, right? Her belly twisted at the thought. Victim? In all her life she'd never been a victim, and she wasn't about to start now. Her pride surged. "I'm just down the block."

"Good. Then it's no big deal if I walk with you."

The man was insufferable. She stomped her foot, her temper getting the best of her. "Don't you know it's not polite to stalk? It's like, a legit crime."

"I'm pretty sure it pales in comparison to armed robbery," he returned, pulling his hands from his pockets and crossing his arms over his broad chest. He had another think coming if he thought he could intimidate her. It was so *not* going to work. "I'm doing this, so you might as well accept it."

"Whatever." Turning on her heel, she started down the block. The sooner she got home, the sooner she could send her pushy escort packing. "This is ridiculous. I was born and raised in the city. I can take care of myself, thank you very much."

"Give me your shopping bag," he ordered, extending his hand expectantly. The only thing she was giving him was the side eye, which only seemed to encourage him further, judging by the shit-eating grin on his face. "I'll carry it for you."

"I'm perfectly capable of carrying my own bag."

Maybe she was being difficult, but he was a certified pain in the ass.

Besides, she'd never admit that it was kind of sweet he'd offered to carry her bag.

Or that, for the first time, she was unnerved at the prospect of walking home through the deserted streets alone.

Victim. The word kept echoing in her brain and she didn't like the way it made her feel. Not. One. Bit.

Reaching out, he grasped the handle of her reusable shopping bag, forcing her to give it up. "It's the least I can do after you saved my ass back there."

"Damn straight. And don't you forget it," she grumbled, resigned to her fate. Maybe letting Ryan walk her home wasn't such a bad idea after all. Of course, she'd bathe in hot coals before acknowledging it. "Speaking of which, I cannot believe the cashier gave you that stupid lime for free. If anyone deserved free groceries, it was me."

His eyebrows shot up. "I don't know. Maybe she likes..." He paused, looking uncharacteristically unsure of himself. "Lumberjacks?"

Was he going to say something else? Did it even matter?

They walked in silence for a while, the tension between them thick and wrought with something fiery she couldn't quite name. The snow was accumulating fast, growing deeper with each fluffy white flake drifting from the sky.

Normally she loved the snow, but tonight? It was wreaking havoc on her life.

"Why does it have to be so freaking cold?" She wrapped her arms around herself, trying to ward off the chill.

"You should wear a hat to help retain body heat. And it would keep you dry." He brushed snow from the collar of her coat, catching her off guard with the familiar gesture.

When his fingers grazed the sensitive skin at the base of her neck, heat blazed through her, warming her from the inside out.

"What about you?" she asked, ignoring the sudden spike in body temperature. No way was she getting hot for this man. "It's like ten degrees out here and you're strutting around with no coat. What, are you from the North Pole?"

It would certainly explain the scruff that lined his chin, making him look like even more of a Neanderthal. Yeah, Ryan definitely wasn't her type. Even though it was sort of a turn-on how he'd tried to be the hero earlier. Plenty of guys, especially the ones she dated, would've turned a blind eye, too worried about their fancy shoes and pretty faces to step in, even with a woman in trouble.

"Very funny. I'm from Minnesota." He shrugged as if that explained it all. "The cold doesn't bother me much."

"Well, this is me," she said, stopping in front of her building and turning to face him.

A dusting of snow covered his shoulders and the tips of his hair, softening the big, hard man in front of her. Should she invite him up? Offer him a drink? What was protocol for a near death situation among strangers?

Before she could overthink it, he took the decision out of her hands.

His lips descended upon hers, gentle at first, but growing hungry and desperate when she stretched up on her toes and kissed him back. Opening herself to him, she took the kiss deeper, tangling her fingers in his damp hair and pulling him closer. It was hot and cold and hard and soft all at once.

Everything she'd expected and nothing she'd imagined.

Unable to process the conflicting feelings, her brain shorted out from sensory overload.

He snaked his arms around her back, gripping her ass and pulling her body flush to him as her tongue mated with his, caressing and massaging in response to his dominating thrusts. She was vaguely aware that he'd lifted her from her feet and the realization sent white-hot need tearing through her. The groan that rolled from his lips confirmed that he also craved more.

Sucking his lower lip, she teased him mercilessly, enjoying the taste of spearmint on his breath.

When they finally broke apart, she was breathless, gasping at the icy cold air that filled her lungs but did nothing to mitigate the scorching hot lust burning up her skin. "I'm Chloe, by the way."

"Nice to meet you, Chloe." He grinned, looking entirely too pleased with himself. "You should know I've wanted to do that from the moment I first saw you."

For the second time that evening, she found herself speechless.

That kiss? It had been seductive, and sweet, and mind-blowing.

And jackass or not, she kind of wanted another one.

She couldn't remember the last time she'd been so thoroughly kissed. Probably never.

The guys she normally dated were a little lacking in the passion department. She'd never kissed a man with facial hair before and she was surprised to discover she didn't hate it. There was something very masculine about the way it scratched her face, no doubt leaving her lips red and swollen.

Oh, who was she kidding? Everything about him was masculine.

It wasn't just his size. It was his protective nature. He was a throwback to another age.

With a little encouragement, he'd probably throw her over his shoulder, tote her upstairs, and screw her eight ways to Sunday.

She just had to say the word.

Too bad she'd sworn off men just an hour ago.

She was over them. Completely. Totally. Over them.

On the other hand, she didn't feel like being alone tonight. What harm could come from one little drink? Or one more kiss, for that matter? They'd been through hell. They deserved it, didn't they?

The words were on her lips before she could stop them. "Come up for a drink?"

He followed her up to her apartment, quiet as a mouse.

A really big, hulking mouse who oozed testosterone.

Once inside, she shrugged off her coat and headed straight to the kitchen. After that little firestorm, she needed a drink more than ever.

"So, why are you dressed up anyway?" he asked, looking totally at home in her tiny apartment and making the space seem even tighter than usual. "Going to a party?"

"Hardly." She pulled a bottle of Jose and a shaker from the cabinet. "I was supposed to be on a date tonight, but the douche canoe blew me off via text. Thus the margaritas. Lime?"

Their fingers brushed as he handed over the fruit, unleashing a flurry of butterflies in her belly. "A text?" he asked, incredulous. "Are you shitting me?"

"Afraid not. I don't know about you, but I plan to get lit up like a Christmas tree," she said, refusing to feel bad about it. "And then I'm swearing off men indefinitely."

"That's a shame." He devoured her with his eyes, his gaze lingering on her curves, appreciating all the parts she'd wished to change a thousand times over. Another wave of arousal crashed through her. "And for what it's worth, he's a fool."

Maybe she'd been too hasty in swearing off men, because Ryan the Jerk was looking pretty damn fine. And judging by the dampness in her panties, her body wholeheartedly agreed.

6

RYAN

RYAN WATCHED while Chloe quickly and efficiently mixed their drinks. His gaze travelled the small apartment, taking in the cozy, lived in feel of the place. Despite the chill creeping through the ancient living room window, it actually felt warm, like a real home. The walls were covered with pictures, the floor littered with shoes.

It suited her larger-than-life personality.

It was also the complete opposite of his sterile apartment, which his ex-girlfriend had decorated to mirror a Pottery Barn centerfold. Half the time, he felt guilty sitting on his own damn couch, like he was going to ruin the place just by living in it.

Dumping all thoughts of his ex, he stepped up to the bar where Chloe was slicing the lime like a pro. She was perfectly at ease in the kitchen, something he hadn't expected. After all, she was more Kim Kardashian than Martha Stewart.

"You're pretty good with a knife."

She raised her brow and laughed. "I can't cook worth a damn, but I make a mean drink. It put me through school. You name it, I can mix it."

"Really? What self-respecting bartender uses a pre-made mixer?" he asked, even though he could picture it clearly.

With her attitude, she'd be a great bartender, taking no shit from the drunk guys who were sure to spend all night hitting on her and ogling those perfect breasts. Or that ass. It wasn't exactly a leap to imagine her rolling around in his sheets with that little pinup body.

She might look prim and proper with her fancy dress and upturned nose, but he'd wager there was a very naughty girl under that refined exterior.

With a mouth like hers? He'd bet his salary on it.

"The store was out of lime juice." She dipped two glasses in salt and poured their drinks, finishing both with a slice of fruit. "And limes."

Totally oblivious to the impact the gesture was having on him, she licked the excess salt from her fingertips. Like it or not, she had his undivided attention now, his cock coming to life, his balls tightening at the sight of her laving the tiny crystals from her fingers.

What kind of asshole would dump a girl like this over text message?

Probably one of those slick metrosexual types that were so predominant in the city. That would be about right. One of those self-important pricks with a cashmere scarf and his initials embroidered on his shirt sleeves.

Was that the kind of guy she usually went for?

Probably, judging by her cocktail dress and elaborately styled hair.

Then again, did it matter? Neither of them was looking for anything long term, but what was to stop them from having one night? Right here, right now.

Fuck it. He was overthinking the situation.

Despite the many names she'd called him, it was pretty

damn clear she was physically attracted to him. Maybe they could pound out their mutual frustration in the bedroom.

Only he had no intention of taking her to bed.

Stepping around the bar, he joined her in the kitchen, purposefully crowding her in the tiny space.

Hand shaking, she reached for her drink. He captured her wrist, surprised again by how small she was next to him. When she looked up, the fire in her eyes said it all. The urge to make her forget about her shitty day overwhelmed every other thought in his brain.

This woman needed a man to worship her and he could be that man for one night.

Hell, with those curves, it would be his pleasure.

"Let's cut to the chase. You didn't really invite me up here for drinks."

"Oh, really?" she challenged, tilting her nose in the air and slipping back into the sarcasm she wore like second skin. "Because no woman can possibly resist Eau de Lumberjack?"

"If the flannel shirt fits." Ryan grinned and rubbed his thumb across the tender flesh on the underside of her wrist. Her protests weren't fooling him. Like a stick of dynamite, she was burning hot under all that bravado. "After all, you did try to climb me like a tree downstairs."

"You're an ass," she breathed, her body shifting almost imperceptibly closer. He skimmed his free hand over her collarbone, finding her skin soft and supple, just as he'd imagined. A nervous laugh rolled off her lips. "Fine. You're such an expert on women. Why don't you tell me what it is you think I want?"

"Right now?" Ryan studied her, deciding to play it straight. His next words would either drive her wild with lust or get him thrown out on his ass. Only one way to find out what kind of woman Chloe really was under all that prim and proper polish.

"Right now you want me to fuck you so dirty the only thing you will be able to think of—*the only thing you will care about*—will be your next orgasm. The first of many I'm going to give you tonight."

Her breath hitched in her throat, breasts rising and falling with the action. Those coffee-colored eyes of hers grew even darker, curiosity and hunger churning in their depths as she silently contemplated him.

Unable to bear Chloe's silence, and needing another taste of her sweet skin, he licked the sensitive flesh of her neck. The sigh that followed confirmed her arousal.

He placed a delicate kiss in the same spot. "Am I right princess?"

Chloe nodded, unable or more likely unwilling to voice her consent.

Not good enough. When she broke apart with pleasure, it would be because she asked for it. Wanted it. Needed it.

Just like he needed her underneath him, screaming his name.

Ryan shifted, pinning her to the counter and pressing his hips against her, letting her feel the length of his erection on her belly. The woman had him so fucking hard he was going to lose his mind. "I need to hear you say it."

"I want you to fuck me dirty. Right here on the counter." A mischievous grin lit up her face. "And Ryan? I want it so dirty I forget everything, even my own name."

"The only name you'll have on your lips is mine," he growled, determined to make good on the promise. "That little gold dress of yours is driving me fucking crazy. I need to tear it off and find out what's underneath."

With a flick of the wrist, she reached back and unzipped the dress.

The slow drag of the zipper was torture.

She was toying with him. He knew it right down to his aching balls, which were so tight he'd probably lose it as soon as he got inside her.

When the dress finally fell to the floor, pooling around her feet, he wanted to thank the dumbass who'd dumped her tonight.

Holy fuck. The sight before him was better than any pinup fantasy he'd ever indulged. Under the dress she wore a lacy black slip with a garter belt that connected to lace topped stockings.

It was sexiest damn thing he'd seen in ages.

"What are you waiting for, Lumberjack Boy?"

"Is that a challenge?" He seized her hips and boosted her onto the counter, making them more evenly matched in height and giving him an unobstructed view of her full breasts. Reaching around, he pulled the clip from her hair, freeing a mass of unruly curls. He tugged on one, watching with interest as it sprang back when released. "Trust me on this, princess. You'll enjoy it a hell of a lot more if I take my time. And I plan to take all night."

She rolled her eyes. "Promises, promises."

Grabbing her chin, he forced her to look him in the eye. "I always keep my promises."

If she knew nothing else about him, she'd know that much by the time they were through.

He ran his hands down the outside of her thighs, enjoying the silky feel of her stockings sliding under his fingers. Her sharp intake of breath suggested that despite her eye-rolling sarcasm, she wanted this as badly as he did. When he reached her knees, he reversed, palms traveling up her inner thighs, spreading her legs for him. She was fully exposed except for the small scrap of black satin that shielded her body.

Drawing on years of discipline, he stopped short of his final destination, pausing to massage the bare skin between her slip and stockings.

She held her breath while he kneaded the soft flesh, no doubt waiting for him to move on to her panties. But he'd meant what he said. He had no intention of rushing, even if he did have the mother of all hard-ons.

With the storm raging outside, they had all night to explore one another, and as much as he wanted her, the foreplay would only intensify their mutual pleasure.

He grabbed a piece of ice from the tray she'd been using to make margaritas. "We're going to play a game," he said, holding the ice cube up for inspection.

"With ice?" She furrowed her brow, not looking the least bit interested. "It's freezing!"

"Trust me." Turning her wrist over, he rubbed the ice cube over the thin skin on the underside. She shivered on contact, her entire body trembling from the chill. Goose bumps ran up her arm. Bringing her wrist to his mouth, he licked the wet spot, sucking hard on the tender skin. She gasped at the heat of his lips, a sharp contrast to the ice. "Everywhere this ice cube goes, my mouth follows."

Her dark eyes were ripe with desire as she contemplated the rules. Finally, she nodded, accepting his terms. "I like this game already."

"I thought you would." A smiled tugged at his lips. There were a lot of games he could teach a woman with her adventurous spirit. "Now be a good girl and hold out your arm."

She did as instructed, a look of anticipation on her face as she watched him, waiting to see what he'd do next. Her bottom wriggled against the counter. He wanted to touch her, see if she was wet, but once he plunged into her, he'd lose what little control he had. Instead he moved the ice cube up her inner arm, following it with a trail of kisses that left them both breathless.

Next, he started behind her ear, dragging the ice cube down her neck and pausing at the hollow between her breasts.

"Don't you dare stop," she said, whimpering in anticipation. Her chest heaved as she sucked in a deep breath. The hot flesh brushed his cheek, tempting him.

"Wouldn't dream of it, princess." Like he could stop if he wanted to. Returning to her ear, he sucked the lobe into his mouth and bit down. Her cry of pain melted into a sigh of pleasure when his tongue darted out, massaging the sting away. Then he nibbled his way back to the sweet mounds demanding his attention. The way her breasts strained against the restrictive lace? It was fucking torture. Ryan licked his lips and brought his gaze to her face. Chloe's wild eyes locked with his, communicating her unspoken need. "Show me."

For once, she didn't argue, just unhooked her stockings and pulled the slip over her head, freeing her breasts as he'd commanded. And holy mother they were perfect—full and heavy, the rosy peaks puckered and ready.

She arched her back, offering herself to him.

Tracing lazy circles around her left breast, he slowly made his way to the hardened nipple. The ice cube grazed the sensitive bud, and she rose up once again. Ryan dropped his mouth to the cool flesh, his teeth closing over the perfect little mound. Then he bit her. Harder this time. She yelped in response, twisting her fingers in his hair. Asserting control, she forced him to take her deeper. He flicked her nipple with his tongue, following the same path he'd used for the ice.

The resulting moan urged him on.

"On your back," he ordered, placing a hand on her belly and forcing her to lie down on the breakfast bar.

Putting the ice cube aside, he grabbed the thin strings of her bikini underwear and started to pull them down before changing his mind. Lowering himself between her thighs, he blew a hot breath against her panties. Then he licked them, giving her one long, torturously slow drag of his tongue up the center of the already damp fabric.

She squirmed on her back, pushing her hips off the counter. "Take them off. For the love of God, I'm begging you."

"That's not begging, princess." He raised an eyebrow, looking right into her frustrated eyes. "If you were begging, you'd have said please."

She glared at him. "*Please* take my fucking panties off."

He grinned in spite of himself as he pulled her panties down, leaving her stockings in place. Those were staying on. He wanted all that silk wrapped around him when he buried himself in that sweet pussy.

Pushing her thighs wide, he gave himself an unobstructed view of her. She was so fucking wet.

A tortured groan escaped his lips, but he'd made a promise. No rushing.

He ran the ice cube up her thigh.

It was hard to tell if the resulting shudder was from arousal or the return of the cold as it wet her stocking. Dropping to his knees, he settled between her legs, blowing a hot breath on her clit. Giving her no time to prepare for the change in temperature, he put the ice cube against the small nub, and rotated it. She gave a sharp hiss, legs clenching around his head as she bucked off the counter. His mouth followed immediately. Sucking hard at the tiny pleasure center, he worked her with his tongue.

"*Ohh!* That feels..." The words trailed off on a sob. Her hands gripped the edge of the counter, seeking purchase as her hips leaped skyward. "Oh, wow. That feels so freaking good. Do it again. Please," she begged breathlessly. "I need it, Ryan. I'm dying here."

Repeating the move, he used his tongue to apply more

pressure. Determined to push her over the edge, he thrust his fingers inside her, moving them in unison with her writhing hips. It didn't take long. She was primed and ready. Her muscles tightened around him. She screamed his name, coming apart noisily as the orgasm rocked her tiny body.

When he climbed to his feet, Chloe met him with a lazy grin, pushing herself into an upright position. She grabbed the hem of his thermal shirt and yanked it up over his head, taking the flannel shirt with it.

"That's better." She bit her lip, eyes traveling over the muscles of his chest and arms. Her gaze lingered on the newly acquired phoenix tattoo that covered his left shoulder, snaking down his arm to create a sleeve. Then she moved on, her fingers fluttering over his bare skin, leaving a trail of fire in their wake. "Make that *much* better."

Reaching for his belt, she unfastened the buckle with nimble fingers, shoving his pants and boxer briefs down, releasing his throbbing dick. She took him in hand, stroking his shaft and rubbing her thumb across the head, using the pearly bead she found there for lubrication. Unable to control himself, he pumped his hips into her hand, nearly reaching orgasm with two quick strokes.

Sweet Jesus. He needed to be inside this woman—*now*.

Pulling her in for a kiss, he coaxed her forward with a tug of the hips.

Answering his unspoken command, she pressed her breasts against him and scooted to the edge of the counter. His cock found her slick center immediately, the head pushing against her, seeking entry.

"Condom." He pulled away and dug a foil square out of his wallet, rolling it on quickly. "Ready?"

She smirked. "Sweetie, I'm beyond ready. Don't hold back."

Thrusting into her with one fluid stroke, he seated himself deep. And oh, was it tight.

Her sharp inhalation gave him pause. Holding her close, he remained still, giving her time to adjust to his size.

She rolled her hips. Once. Twice. So slow. So incredibly slow. And hard. The friction of her body hugging his cock was going to make him come before she was ready. He needed to move. Needed to feel the slide of her body around him as their hips crashed together.

The third time she let out a veritable purr, and he knew she was toying with him again, waiting to see what it would take to break him.

Without warning, he pulled out.

She gasped at the loss of contact, her lips settling into a disappointed pout.

Angling his hips upward, he slammed back into her. There would be no stopping this time. They would go all the way, coming together. Digging her nails into his shoulders, she matched his pace, rocking her hips and panting with the effort.

"That's it, princess. Ride my cock like a good girl. I need to feel that sweet pussy of yours come again. Can you do that for me?"

"Yes," she moaned, wrapping her silky legs around him. "I'm almost there."

Thank God. He was about to blow and there was no way he was going to come without her. Two more quick strokes and she was screaming his name as he succumbed to his own orgasm, her tight walls milking every last drop he had to offer.

7

CHLOE

CHLOE WATCHED with satisfaction as the kids from Garden of Dreams skated onto the ice at Madison Square Garden. Well, maybe skating was a bit too generous a word for it. Most of them had never even been on skates before and there was a lot of falling, but there was a lot of laughter, too.

The kids were having a blast, which would be great for the photo shoot.

If they were this excited about being on the ice, they'd be beside themselves when the Rangers arrived.

Pacing the rug that had been placed on the ice for suits like herself, she began strategizing.

Landing the Garden of Dreams charity as a client had been a big win for PBA and she was thrilled Cole had assigned her to the campaign. He expected her social media expertise to be an asset, translating to more publicity and ultimately, more funding. Bottom line, PBA needed to fill the coffers with donations by year-end. Although she was excited about the opportunity, there was no denying the crushing weight that had settled on her shoulders as a result.

The foundation was counting on her, and the last thing she wanted to do was let the kids down. Whatever it took, she had to make the campaign a success. After all, wasn't that what she'd promised herself? That she'd put her love life on the back burner and focus on something worthwhile for a change?

Problem was, she was still trying to piece herself back together from those mind-blowing orgasms Ryan had given her Friday night.

Thank God it was a one-shot deal.

No way could she handle more than one night of hot sex with that man. And didn't it just figure that the most infuriating man she'd met in all her life was actually a sex god in disguise?

She was pretty sure he'd ruined her for any other man with that pleasure-giving body of his. He'd marked her for life, leaving her with memories no other man could live up to.

Hell, she was getting turned on just thinking about him.

Which was exactly why she needed to forget about their night together and focus on her job.

She scanned the arena, spotting Cole on the far side of the rink. Common sense told her he was there to meet the Rangers, not check up on her work, but seeing him onsite was all the motivation she needed to clear her head. The man might be her friend Olivia's knight in shining armor, but from eight to five, he was also the boss.

Squaring her shoulders, she went to work.

The next fifteen minutes were spent sharing her vision for the shoot with the photographers. The real trick would be getting the kids, who currently looked as if they'd been mainlining Pixy Stix, settled enough to do their testimonials. That was why she'd convinced the photographers it was best to let them skate for a while and then meet the players.

If she was lucky, they'd burn off some energy before transitioning into the serious stuff.

Halfway through her review of the cue cards, the kids started going wild, screaming and howling. Unable to concentrate, she glanced up to see the Rangers filing out of the players tunnel and joining the kids on the ice. Their excitement was contagious, and she found herself smiling right along with them.

An experience like this would leave a lasting impression on these kids, hopefully changing some of their lives for the better.

The Rangers did a quick lap around the rink, moving at breakneck speed, which only made the kids scream louder, shouting the names of their favorite players, vying for their attention and cheering them to victory in the impromptu race. As the players came full circle and skated to center ice to meet their pintsized fans, one face stood out among the rest.

Son. Of. A. Bitch!

No way. No *freaking* way.

This could not be happening. She blinked, hoping her eyes were playing a dirty trick on her. But no, there he was. Clean shaven. Hot. And wearing a Rangers jersey.

Ryan.

Ryan Douglas, apparently.

There was a very real possibility she was going to die of embarrassment.

Or melt into a puddle of goo right there on the damn rug.

Much as she hated to admit it, he looked even better than she remembered, gliding across the ice in all his perfect male glory.

Lust pooled in her belly. It didn't help that she knew exactly how lickable his sinewy body was underneath that uniform. Strong arms, muscular chest, and her personal favorite, V-cut abs. What wasn't to like? The man was ripped. His shaggy hair brushed the collar of his jersey, and his crooked nose suddenly seemed even sexier, if that was possible. How had he broken it? Stray puck? Elbow? Fight?

No, wait. That was so *not* the point.

What the hell? They weren't supposed to see each other again. *Ever.*

There was only one logical explanation. Clearly the universe hated her. She was being punished for breaking her no sex rule five seconds after swearing off men.

Stop! Don't freak out, she coached herself. Maybe if she kept her head down and her mouth shut, he wouldn't see her. The players were totally focused on the kids, who were sure to keep them busy for the next hour. She'd just lay low and—

"Hey, Chloe!"

Damn. Her head shot up, searching for the source.

"Chloe! We need some advice over here. Got a minute?"

She waved to Becca, her Garden of Dreams liaison, hoping to shut her up before she attracted the attention of everyone in the tri-state area, namely Ryan. Sneaking a peek in his direction, she found his gaze locked on her like a heat-seeking missile.

Double damn.

Pretending not to see him, she joined Becca and the other PR guys, answering their questions and focusing on her job. Every menial little task. Every minute detail. Anything to avoid thinking about that night. About Ryan.

Although she was doing her best to ignore him, she could feel his eyes on her as he worked with the kids. The slow burn that crept up the back of her neck was a dead giveaway. No matter how hard she tried, it was impossible to shut him out.

Hell, hot under the collar didn't even begin to describe her current situation.

When she couldn't take it for another second, and she thought her hair might actually go up in flames, she cracked.

Abandoning all pretense, Chloe watched Ryan glide across

the ice backward, the kids giggling and swiping at him with their sticks, doing their best to steal the puck.

Much as she hated to admit it, he was good with them and the smile on his face suggested he was having as much fun as they were.

She cut her eyes at the photographers. They were eating it up. At least they'd have plenty of material to use for the campaign.

Returning her gaze to her iPad, she watched from under her lashes as Ryan and a couple of the other players attempted to teach the kids to pass a puck. She grinned. It was a complete disaster.

They were too excited to take direction and the pucks were flying all over the place.

But everyone was having fun and that was the only thing that mattered.

Too bad the more she watched Ryan with the kids, the more pissed off she got, realizing she'd probably been a big freaking joke to him. She was the only one in the stupid store that hadn't recognized him. It all made sense now.

The free groceries.

The cops falling all over themselves to take his statement.

His hesitation to explain when she asked him about it.

Not only was Ryan a hockey player, but judging by the big ol' C on his chest, he was also the freaking team captain. God, she was such a fool. And probably the only person in the whole damn city who didn't know his name or his face.

Why would she? She didn't give a crap about hockey, and really, things like this didn't happen to girls like her. Why would someone as sinfully hot and famous as Ryan Douglas have sex with her anyway? Especially after she'd told him about her broken date.

Humiliation burned her cheeks.

Two words came to mind, and try as she might, she couldn't chase them away.

Pity fuck.

8

RYAN

At the sound of Chloe's name, Ryan found himself doing a double take, scanning the arena for her face. After the night they'd shared? Hell, his cock did a double take, too, hoping for an encore performance. And against all odds, there she was, prancing around in a tight little black skirt and a pair of sky-high red fuck me heels that should have been outlawed. She wore her hair down, her curls looking as wild as they had when she'd been coming for him Friday night.

An image of her climaxing on the kitchen counter, hips rocking, lips parted, flashed through his mind, making his shorts uncomfortably tight.

He shifted his weight and his train of thought. What was she doing at The Garden anyway?

Not that he was complaining. The view from the ice had just gotten a hell of a lot better.

It had occurred to him they might bump into one another at the corner store again, but he'd never imagined she might show up here.

He leaned on his stick, watching as she buzzed around

giving orders and doing her damndest to avoid his stare, focusing her attention everywhere but the ice.

He'd rectify that situation soon enough, but first he had some fans to meet.

"Hey, Jordy!" he yelled to one of his linemen, tapping his stick on the ice. "Why don't we show these kids how to pass and see if we've got any future Rangers in the group?"

The kids cheered and repeated his move, signaling they, too, were ready to receive the puck.

Ryan grinned, feeding off their excitement. Being team captain was about more than just leading the guys on the ice and scoring goals. It was about being a good role model and giving back to the community, something he enjoyed immensely. Especially when he got to work with kids.

After all, it wasn't that long ago he was in their shoes, just hoping to make his dream a reality. Of course, he'd had far more advantages than these kids, growing up as he had with two parents who had the means and willingness to support his dream of playing pro hockey.

He'd been damn lucky, which was another reason he took his responsibility to the community, and these kids, seriously.

Jordy flipped him the puck, which he received with ease, letting it crack hard against his stick as he cradled it.

He spent the next hour teaching the fundamentals of the game, but he never lost sight of Chloe. Hell, his cock wouldn't let him forget her presence, even if he wanted to. Fate had dropped her on the rink and he'd be damned before he let the opportunity pass, especially since she seemed hell-bent on ignoring him.

When the time came for a water break, he broke away from the group, skating directly to the spot where she stood tapping away on her tablet like she was pissed at the world.

"Hey, princess. Do I need to remind you that stalking is against the law?"

Those angry little fingers froze on the screen. Her chest rose and fell, her full breasts taunting him. Finally, she looked up, her dark eyes shining under the bright lights of the arena.

"Am I being punk'd?" She frowned, her pinched lips leaving no doubt as to how she felt about the prospect. Her eyes skated over his face, taking in the sweat dripping down his brow. Her breath came fast and furious. From anger? The cold? Something else entirely? "You cannot be a pro hockey player!"

"Why not?" he asked, a smile playing on his lips. Unable to decide if he should be offended by her assumption or flattered, he decided to just go with it. "Give me one good reason."

"Because you still have all your teeth and I can spell your last name!" She poked him in the chest for good measure, which was just ridiculous, considering he towered over her in his pads and skates. He threw his head back and laughed, drawing the attention of the photographers. "Look, you've had your fun, screwing the clueless girl in the furry boots, now leave me alone. I'm done being the butt of your joke or a pity fuck or whatever it was. I'm working," she whisper-yelled through clenched teeth.

Was she serious? She must think he was a first-class asshole.

He tried to see it from her perspective and realized nothing he said was going to change her mind right here, right now. It hadn't been his intention to mislead her. He'd started to tell her, but something had held him back.

Normalcy.

It was nice being with someone who saw him as a regular guy, and not an NHL star, for a change. It had been a long time since he'd just been Ryan. He sighed. The woman was stubborn as hell, but two could play at that game. The difference was, he didn't care who was watching.

"I'm not leaving until you give me your number."

"Yeah, that's not happening," she said, placing a hand on her hip. "I told you, I'm swearing off men. Especially cocky, arrogant athletes."

"What?" he asked, arching his brow. "Now you have a problem with hockey players?"

She rolled her eyes. "You're a quick one, aren't you?"

"It hasn't exactly been a problem in the past." Hell, most of the women he met were falling all over themselves to bed an NHL player. Oh, they didn't come right out and say it, but they didn't have to. Sometimes actions spoke louder than words. Tamping down his irritation, Ryan leaned in close, ensuring that only she could hear his next words. They were so close he could smell her perfume, a sensual floral blend with a sweet edge that got his blood thrumming harder than any lap around the rink ever could. "That was before I ate that beautiful pussy of yours, which, if I remember correctly, you thor-*o*-ughly enjoyed."

Chloe's jaw nearly hit the ice. Her cheeks were flaming, and if looks could kill, he'd have been a goner. Unfortunately for her, he'd never been one to give up easily. Not when he wanted something, and right now he wanted to get this woman on her back screaming his name.

"Look, sweetie, the other night was fun, but it was a one-time thing. You know, because of the feels and whatnot from being in a high stress situation," she finished, turning shuttered eyes on him. Which of them she was trying to convince with her little speech? Maybe she'd been more affected by their night together than she cared to admit. She ran a hand through her hair, as if maintaining that prim and polished look of hers could erase all the dirty things they'd done to one another in her kitchen. "Garden of Dreams is a really important account for me and I need to look good, so get your ass back over there and play captain of the Neanderthals for the kids."

"Not until you give me your number." He leaned on his stick, letting her know he had no intention of moving.

After six years in a relationship, he'd forgotten how exciting it could be to discover a new lover, especially one as responsive as Chloe. He needed another night with the sexy little vixen in front of him.

One taste hadn't been nearly enough.

She huffed out a breath and crossed her arms. "You've clearly taken one too many shots to the head. Me and you? So not happening."

He swallowed his pride and flashed her the smile his sisters had notoriously dubbed The Panty-Melter. "I'm sorry I didn't tell you I played hockey. It didn't seem important at the time. Let me take you to dinner and make it up to you."

"In case you haven't noticed," she said with a flick of the wrist, "I have an actual job and I can buy my own damn dinner."

Her eyes travelled the rink, settling on a guy in a dark suit who was watching them with interest. Lover? No. By her own admission she'd sworn off men. Boss? Judging by the nervous way she chewed her lower lip, it was a safe bet.

Finally, something he could use. She'd said the account was important to her career. Ryan raised a gloved hand and waved.

The suit waved back, looking pleasantly surprised. Chloe, on the other hand, looked panic stricken.

"What do you think you're doing?"

"Just saying hi." He grinned, enjoying the way she wore her passion on her sleeve. This was going to be a piece of cake. "That your boss? He looks pretty pleased."

The suit gave Chloe a thumbs up.

She snorted. "Yeah, well, he's a man. Of course he'd be impressed by the big famous jock with the *C* on his jersey. I'm pretty sure that's standard with a Y chromosome."

"He'd probably be less impressed if he thought you chased

me off the ice with that smart little mouth of yours. Not to mention the kids' disappointment."

"You wouldn't dare!"

He wouldn't. But she didn't know that. "Wanna find out?"

She pursed her lips, no doubt mentally calling him every name in the book. "Fine."

"Fine?"

"I will go to dinner with you if you get your ass back over there and smile pretty for the camera."

"Try not to sound so excited." He smirked, knowing every snide comment she uttered was just another layer of foreplay that would heighten their pleasure when the time came. "Besides, you never know. Maybe I'll take a puck to the face and you'll be off the hook."

"I should be so lucky," she grumbled as he skated away backward.

"By the way," he said, pointing to her stilettos, "I much prefer those to the boots."

"As if I care." She rolled her eyes and turned her back on him. Then she brought her hand up behind her and gave him a one-fingered salute.

Oh, she cared all right. That unladylike little gesture said it all.

He'd gotten under her skin. *Again.* Maybe he had taken too many shots to the head because there was something about her complete and utter disdain for him that was insanely hot.

Dinner with Chloe would be a night to remember. He'd make sure of it.

9

CHLOE

CHLOE GLANCED IN THE MIRROR, wondering what the hell she was supposed to wear on a date with a pro hockey player? Not that she really cared what Ryan thought. As far as she was concerned, he was an arrogant ape.

She'd only agreed to the stupid date to stave off a scene at The Garden. The last thing she wanted to do was shake Cole's confidence in her, or make him think she wasn't taking the responsibility seriously. So what choice did she have but to accept Ryan's invitation?

After all, he'd practically blackmailed her.

Of course, she could bail on him. It would certainly serve him right.

But no, she refused to sink to his level. She'd just have to suck it up and go. One date wouldn't kill her, and then she'd be done with him once and for all.

Turning to her closet, she grabbed a conservative black cap-sleeved dress. It was more nine-to-five than date-night, but one could never go wrong with a little black dress, right? Even if it was boring.

Hell, the duller the better.

Maybe it would keep Ryan at arm's length, something she desperately needed to do if she wanted to put this whole mess behind her and focus on Garden of Dreams.

Chloe sighed. If she'd had the slightest idea he was an NHL player, she never would have invited him up that first night. And she sure as hell wouldn't have slept with him, nerves or not.

The man embodied everything she despised.

Maybe she didn't know Ryan, but she knew his type. Self-involved, entitled, *fleeting*. He'd have his fun, and when someone shiny and new came along? He'd drop her in a New York minute.

She slipped the dress over her head, shimmying into it and pulling the skirt over her butt. A devious plan sprouted in her brain as she tugged it down to a respectable length.

Pulling the dress back over her head, she tossed it on the bed.

She pushed aside all the suits in her closet, rummaging in the back, searching for the little red dress that was anything but boring. A satin fit and flare with a plunging neckline in the front and back, it was sure to make Ryan lose his mind.

He wanted to play games? Fine by her. She just hoped he was prepared to lose, because she was all in.

Only she had no intention of giving up the goods.

He could look, but there would be no touching. Not this time.

Finishing the dress with a pair of black fishnet stockings, black booties, and a thick black belt, she studied her reflection in the mirror.

Game. On.

Although he'd wanted to pick her up like a proper gentleman, Chloe had shot him down, insisting they meet at the restaurant. And the sooner she got out the door, the sooner this little battle of wills would be over.

When she arrived, she checked her coat and allowed the hostess to escort her to the table where she was told Ryan was already waiting. She'd insisted on choosing the restaurant, making sure it was a lively one with a hopping bar. It wasn't quiet or romantic or exclusive and she wouldn't have to worry about things heating up. Added bonus, it wasn't so over the top she'd have to worry about which fork to use or whether the server was judging the shit out of her.

Damn.

The joke was on her because Ryan looked good enough to eat and apparently the slender blonde hovering near the table agreed. She was eyeing him like he was the only thing on the menu worth having.

Maybe she should have bailed after all. It didn't look like he'd miss her.

Just as she was about to turn and walk out, he looked up, catching her eye.

"Chloe!" He stood, dismissing the other woman, his attention completely focused on her. His eyes traveled over her body, taking in the racy dress, which hugged her curves as she approached the table. When his eyes fell on the fishnet stockings, his grin widened. Leaning in, he gave her a kiss on the cheek and whispered in her ear. "I was starting to think you weren't going to show."

"You mean because you blackmailed me into coming? No, just fashionably late." She gave him a tight-lipped smile, cutting her eyes at the back of the blonde who was retreating to the bar. "Hopefully I'm not interrupting."

"Hardly." He smirked, his overinflated ego no doubt mistaking her irritation for jealousy. Not missing a beat, he leaned down into her personal space again as he helped her into her chair. "There's only one woman I'm interested in, and she's wearing a pair of stockings that are going to make it damn near impossible to think about anything but having them wrapped around me later tonight."

Flustered, Chloe grabbed the drink menu. Refusing to meet his eyes, she stared at it like a coward until the server arrived, the whole time willing herself not to use it as a fan.

She ordered a glass of red wine, reminding herself she was in control, not Ryan.

So he liked her stockings? Perfect. That was the point, wasn't it? To drive him mad with lust and send him and his blue balls packing.

She just had to hang tough and not let her stupid hormones get the best of her.

She. Had. This.

Too bad his eyes were still smoldering, heavy with lust, when she looked up.

It didn't take a genius to figure out he was imaging all the ways he might fuck her.

He thought he could stare her down? That just wouldn't do. No way was she backing down.

She took a sip from her water glass, drawing an ice cube into her mouth and gliding it across her lower lip where he could see it. Then she sucked on that thing like it was her job, working it with her tongue.

There was an audible hiss from Ryan's side of the table. He shifted in his seat.

And was it her imagination or was his breath just a bit more labored?

A flash caught her off guard and she damn near choked on the stupid ice cube.

Ryan turned toward the flash and smiled, only it didn't quite reach all the way to his eyes.

"Ryan," the photographer said, snapping another pic, "how's the leg? Think you'll be able to make the comeback?"

"The leg's good. Doc cleared me to practice this week. I'll be back in the game before you know it."

"Think you'll be able to play the Flyers?" the photog asked, firing questions nonstop like he didn't really give a crap about the answers and just needed sound bites.

"We'll see." Ryan gripped his beer so hard his knuckles turned white. "They're a formidable rival. I hope to be back on the ice, supporting the team in any way I can."

The paparazzo looked at Chloe, his skeezy eyes locked on her chest. *Dirtball.* She couldn't remember the last time a guy actually made her skin crawl. "Who's your friend?"

"A friend," Ryan replied, his body going rigid.

It was pretty clear to Chloe that he was done talking, but the pap opened his mouth to ask another question.

"How's Kel—"

Fortunately, the restaurant manager came rushing over and politely, but firmly, kicked the guy out before he could finish his impromptu interview.

"I'm so sorry," she said, looking horrified as she clutched a stack of menus to her chest. "That should never have happened. We do value our guest's privacy. I'll speak with the hostess."

"Thank you." Ryan released his glass and Chloe swore she could actually see the tension leak out of his shoulders.

She was very aware that every eye in the place was trained on their table. She forced a smile, doing her best to look unfazed. Sure, why not? Paparazzi taking her picture during a night on the town, invading her privacy?

Nothing new about that. Happened all the time.

Only it probably did happen to Ryan all the time she realized, and vowed to delete the TMZ app from her phone.

"Your dinner is on us tonight," the manager offered with an awkward grin. "Please enjoy the rest of your evening. You won't be bothered again."

"So, that was fun," Chloe said, trying to ignore the fact that half the people in the place were probably talking about them.

Ryan shook his head, a ghost of a smile on his lips. For the first time since she'd met him, he wasn't the cocky bastard who taunted her mercilessly. She saw something different on his face: vulnerability.

"I'm really sorry about that."

"Does it happen a lot?" she asked, wondering what it was like to live under a microscope for all the world to judge.

She didn't want to think about what the world would see if they followed her around for a few days.

Ryan studied her, his eyes penetrating, as if he could read her mind. "Only on slow news days."

"Guess there aren't any Kardashian's in town this week."

His lips twitched. "I guess not. Which makes an injured hockey player today's big story."

"What happened?" she asked, hating that she actually wanted to know more about him. She chalked it up to morbid curiosity, because no way in hell did she actually care.

"The truth? Freak accident. I took a blade to the back of the calf during a Flyers game earlier in the season. It sliced deep." He shrugged as if it were no big deal, but the way he toyed with his beer told a different story. "Two surgeries and a hell of a lot of PT later, I'm well on my way to recovery."

"Oh my God. That's horrible." Her belly churned at the thought of such a gory injury. What he'd been through sounded incredibly painful. It couldn't have been an easy recovery. Watching him today, she'd never have guessed he'd been sidelined with an injury. Then again, playing with a bunch of kids was a far cry from the intensity of a professional game. "I'm so sorry."

He tipped his head back and took a long pull from his beer, throat bobbing as he drained the glass. "I've missed forty-three games. There's a lot of speculation as to whether I'll be able to play again, or if the injury is a career killer."

"But the doc cleared you, right?"

"Yeah." He scrubbed a hand over his face. Doubt clouded his eyes. "Yeah, he did."

"So, fuck 'em. You go back out there and make those haters eat their words."

"It won't be easy."

"Neither is becoming a professional hockey player, so I kind of like your odds."

10

RYAN

Ryan watched Chloe as he signed another autograph. They'd moved to the bar after dinner, deciding to grab a few drinks before calling it a night. Unfortunately, they'd been interrupted no less than a dozen times by well-wishers who wanted his autograph.

Normally he didn't mind, but tonight it was really trying his patience.

To her credit, Chloe was taking it all in stride, chatting with the woman on the stool next to her.

Despite the many interruptions, he was glad she hadn't ditched him. Chloe had a realness about her he hadn't seen much since moving to New York, and it was refreshing. Not only was she spirited, she was authentic. This wasn't a woman interested in his career or how much money he made.

Hell, he wasn't even sure she liked him, despite their sizzling chemistry.

Plus, she had this whole "I call them like I see them" kind of attitude that was proving to be a real turn-on. With her flashy clothes and unfiltered commentary, she really didn't seem to give a fuck what anyone thought, least of all him.

It didn't hurt that the sex was unbelievable either.

"Why so serious?" Chloe turned her stool to face him, crossing her legs and drawing his eyes to her silk covered thighs.

Was she wearing those lacey garters again? He wanted —*needed*—to touch her and find out.

Instead, he replied, "Just thinking about practice on Monday."

She offered him a reassuring smile he didn't deserve. "Don't worry. I'm sure no one expects you to be one hundred percent on your first day back."

"It's not that," he admitted, leaning against the bar so their shoulders were touching. Might as well hit her with the highlights. She was bound to hear about it anyway. "When I got hurt, my girlfriend of six years, Kelsey, dumped me and hooked up with my best friend Bash. Who's also on the team," he explained, remembering she wasn't a hockey fan and could probably count all the Rangers whose names she knew on one finger.

"That bitch!" The look of outrage on her face was priceless.

What did it say about the six years he'd spent with Kelsey that a woman he'd known for six minutes had more respect for him?

"Yeah, well, she wasn't so sure I'd recover, and she didn't want to give up the lifestyle. I haven't seen either of them in a few months." He raked a hand through his hair and stared at his beer. "I'm excited about heading up to the training center on Monday, but it's going to be awkward as hell in the locker room."

"You don't sound too broken up over it."

He looked up. Chloe was watching him with raised brows, making it clear she expected an answer. "I guess I wasn't that surprised. And it wasn't like he stole her away. It was her choice. She just packed her bags and walked out. Deep down I knew we had problems, but I was too wrapped up in the game to deal with them. It was just a matter of time."

"So then what's the problem?"

"The guys on the team will be watching me, waiting to see how I'll handle the situation. I'm a leader and I don't want to tear the team apart, but I can't ignore it either."

She placed a delicate hand on his shoulder. "You, sir, have come to the right place for advice."

He laughed. "Sorry, princess, but we aren't going to hug it out like a couple of chicks."

"Do I look like a hug it out kind of girl?" she asked, feigning indignation. "Trust me. I have three brothers. I'm an expert on dealing with boy drama."

Her breath was hot against his ear as she whispered her plan to him, her lips grazing his jaw and sending a ripple of desire to his cock.

"You have a devious mind. And that is so incredibly sexy."

11

CHLOE

CHLOE EYED the shot of Patron that sat in front of her and decided she was done cutting Ryan a break. She was sympathetic to his injury, the paparazzi, and even his bitchy ex-girlfriend, but she wasn't letting him off the hook entirely. He was still an ass. And if he called her—

"Half-pint princess, are you sure you can handle that shot?" he asked, his eyes dancing with laughter. He leaned over, crowding her with his massive body.

Heat radiated from him, and thanks to her choice of dress, she was annoyingly aware of it, craving to touch that feverish skin of his. The man had balls, she'd give him that much at least.

Not only did he have the audacity to blackmail her into this stupid date, now he was making fun of her.

It was time to get back the upper hand.

"Sweetie, I may be small, but I can handle my liquor." She brought his hand to her mouth and licked the stretch of skin between his thumb and forefinger, her tongue darting out seductively. Ryan followed her every move, his eyes glued to her as she sprinkled salt on the slick spot and grabbed a lime. Licking the salt from his hand with a slow drag of her tongue, she slammed the Patron and bit into the lime, sucking on it very deliberately as she withdrew it from her lips. The alcohol burned its way to her belly, taking the edge off her nerves. Trailing a manicured nail down his chest, she pulled out the sexiest smile in her arsenal. "I can go one for one all night long. Can you?"

Something dark stirred in his eyes.

Lust. She was sure of it, even if she didn't understand it.

How the hell was she, Chloe Jacobs, sitting at the bar with one of the sexiest guys in the NHL eye-fucking her?

She had no real basis for comparison, but he was pretty damn fine, so it was a safe bet he was at the top end of the hockey hottie spectrum. Were all hockey players this easy on the eyes?

Ryan swiped her beer and downed it in three quick gulps.

"Hey." Her temper flared hotter than the hinges of hell. "What exactly do you think you're doing?"

He was on her in a flash, spinning her stool and trapping her between his powerful arms, his palms braced on the edge of the bar. The hard muscles of his chest were pressed to her back, a stark contrast to her own soft body. He brought his mouth to her ear, nipping at her earlobe and tracing the inside of her ear with his tongue.

A rush of desire surged through her, reminding her of the need he'd awoken deep within.

She sighed, cursing herself yet again for responding to his touch like an unsatisfied virgin.

"I need you sober enough to say yes when I take you home and fuck you until you go mad thinking your body will come apart with pleasure. The first time will be quick. But after that? It's going to take all night because I'm going to learn every single spot on this body that makes you moan. And I'm going to do it with my tongue."

To prove his point, he swiveled her stool, bringing them face-to-face.

His mouth descended without hesitation, or care for who might be watching.

Or maybe in spite of it.

Those soft lips crashed against hers, driving the kiss deep and hard, their tongues inextricably entwined as she tilted her head back and opened herself to him. He tangled his fingers in her hair, exploring her mouth and tempting her with the promise of more.

When he pulled back, Chloe gasped at the loss of contact.

She was so screwed.

The time for fun and games had passed.

There was only one answer she could give this man. Only one she wanted to give, despite her resolution. But then what? She couldn't even hang onto Dave the Douche.

How could she possibly hope to keep Ryan, the dirty talking, scorching sex god?

She couldn't. It was that simple. Which actually made him kind of perfect.

Forget Mr. Right. Get down and dirty with Mr. Right Now.

No expectations. No emotions. Just a whole lot of sinful pleasure.

Why shouldn't he pound an orgasm out of her, no strings attached?

Sure, he was infuriating with all his swagger and bossiness, but it did nothing to negate their chemistry. And neither of them was looking for long term. By his own admission he'd just gotten out of a crappy relationship, and she was taking a hiatus from getting dumped.

It was perfect, really. Besides, no one had to know.

"My place or yours?" she asked, ignoring the niggling voice

in the back of her head that warned her to walk away while she still could.

"Your place is closer," he said with a sly grin.

They barely made it back to her apartment. A whopping two whole blocks.

By the time they got up the stairs, Ryan was sucking on her neck making it damn near impossible to get the key in the lock. When the door finally swung open, they fell through, joined at the lips. Desperate for him to make good on his promise and put that tongue to good use, she devoured him with hungry kisses.

They crashed into the sideboard, sending the giant stack of mail skittering to the floor. Who cared? She didn't. Pressing her to the wall, he slipped a hand under her skirt, feeling his way to the top of her fishnet stockings. When he grabbed her ass, she lifted her leg, wrapping it around him.

"These are so fucking hot, but they have to go," he said, moving from her mouth to her chin, scraping his teeth along her jawline.

Dropping to his knees, he pulled the pantyhose down, taking her underwear too. She kicked off her shoes and stepped out of the restrictive undergarments, making a mental note to buy more thigh high stockings. There was something to be said for the easy access they provided, and Ryan seemed to like them. He pushed her dress up, eyes locked on her bare, well, *everything*. Only she didn't feel self-conscious.

Hell, the way he was looking at her she felt like the sexiest damn woman in the world.

He could stare all day as far as she was concerned.

Except that it meant they weren't kissing. Or screwing. And what fun was that?

Seizing the front of his shirt, she pulled him to his feet, capturing his mouth on the way up. She nipped at his lower lip, sucking hard. The responsive groan he gave sent a zing of pleasure right to her center. Slipping his arms around her back, he cupped her ass and lifted her in the air. Wrapping her legs around him, she used the leverage to boost herself higher and rubbed her body against his. It was a futile attempt to satisfy the tension coiled low in her belly.

"Bedroom?"

"Thought you'd never ask. Back of the hall," she panted, running her fingers through his silky hair.

He carried her to the bed, laying her down without breaking their connection. Lowering his massive body on top of her, he pinned her to the mattress with his hips. She went straight for the buttons on his shirt, desperate for skin-to-skin contact. Ryan worked her belt, releasing the clasp and dragging the little red dress up over her head, leaving her naked beneath him.

He pulled back, studying her from above.

"You wore this just to torture me with those perfect tits, didn't you?" Shaking his head, he held up the dress. "No bra. I fucking knew it."

Busted.

She smirked, dropping her eyes to the raging hard-on that strained against the front of his jeans. "Looks like it worked."

With his free hand, he caressed her breast, rolling the hardened nipple between his thumb and forefinger. "That's a dangerous game you're playing, princess." He pinched her. The jolt of pleasure/pain sent her senses into overdrive. His mouth followed, sucking the tender flesh and massaging it with his tongue. She wiggled beneath him, needing more. "You should know I always play to win."

Unnerved by the dark look in his eyes, she returned her attention to his shirt.

Peeling it back revealed the well-muscled shoulders she remembered from their first night together. The phoenix tattoo on his shoulder took on new meaning as she caressed it, wondering if Ryan himself would rise from the ashes and return to greatness. Not that it was any of her concern. She pushed the thought aside, running her hands over the corded muscles of his arms. They were working hard to ensure that thick body of his didn't crush her.

It gave her an idea. A very naughty idea.

Ryan liked games? Maybe they weren't done playing after all. Perhaps it was just time to change the rules.

Only this time they'd be in her favor.

"Switch." She pushed him off and rolled him onto his back, climbing atop and straddling him. What would it be like to have all that male power restrained beneath her? She was about find out. "Close your eyes."

He started to argue, but she put a finger to his lips, following it with a light kiss.

When she was sure his eyes were closed, she reached into the nightstand and pulled out the handcuffs she'd bought at Halloween to go with her sexy cop costume. She'd never expected to use them, but the opportunity seemed too good to pass up. This time she'd be in control, and the only person getting tortured would be Ryan. She rotated her hips and stroked his arms, stretching them above his head and putting them in range of the wrought iron headboard.

Then she snapped on the cuffs.

His eyes shot open. "What the fuck!"

The cuffs scraped the headboard as he tried to bring his arms down.

"We're going to play a game," she said, echoing his words from their first night together. "With handcuffs. There's only one rule. I'm in control."

Leaning back, she settled over his hips, giving him full view of her breasts. He could look, but he couldn't touch.

Ryan appraised her as if seeing her for the first time.

Shifting his hips, he relaxed, accepting his fate. "Okay, princess. Your game, your rules. But when I get out of these handcuffs—"

"Baby, I'll fuck you so good you won't ever want to get out of those handcuffs."

And she meant it. She had every intention of riding him until they were both fully spent.

After that? Who cared?

She crawled to the end of the bed and stripped off his jeans. Only his thick erection remained between them. Glowing with the knowledge that *she'd* done that to him, gotten him to that undeniable state of arousal, she repositioned herself over his thighs. He watched intently as she leaned down and blew a hot breath on the head of his cock. The determined set of his jaw suggested he was doing everything in his power not to react. They'd just see about that, wouldn't they?

She licked her lips, moving her tongue over the top one first. No reaction. Then the lower one.

His penis twitched.

Point, Chloe.

"Do you have any idea what I'm going to do to you?" She blew another breath onto his fevered skin, massaging his thighs, avoiding direct contact with his towering erection, just inches from her mouth.

"You're going to wrap those sweet lips around my dick and suck me off, aren't you, princess?"

She stroked his thigh. "Would you like that?"

"I've never wanted it so bad in my life," he growled, shifting his hips again. The urge to take him in her mouth was overwhelming. The idea of reciprocating the pleasure he'd given her was a strong lure. Add to it the rush of having such a big, powerful man handcuffed to her bed and she was practically a goner. "Take me in your mouth."

"Did you forget your manners?" Starting at the base, she stroked his cock with the palm of her hand. "You forgot to say please."

"*Please.*" It was a strangled cry. Taking pity on him, she lowered herself and licked the head. Just one quick little swipe of the tongue.

He moaned, his tortured gaze never leaving her mouth. "Do it again."

This time she happily obliged, her own arousal demanding she quit screwing around and get down to business. Bracing herself on his thighs, she wrapped her fingers around the base of his cock and took him into her mouth, circling the shaft with the tip of her tongue.

"*Fuuuck,*" he groaned, arching his hips and nearly toppling her. "That feels amazing. I need more, baby. Fuck me with your mouth. Make it fast."

Eager to please, she did as he commanded, taking him deep and withdrawing, her tongue desperately working him with each wild thrust of his hips.

"I'm going to come if you keep that up." He rattled the handcuffs. "Get up here and ride me, princess. I want to watch those tits bounce while you're fucking me. I want you to look into my eyes and know who it is that makes you come so hard."

Abandoning her own rules, she delved into the nightstand for a condom. She ripped it open and rolled it on before straddling Ryan again. Hesitating only briefly, she lowered herself, spreading her thighs and taking him deep. Blistering heat tore through her.

It wouldn't take much to send her soaring. Her own climax was close at hand.

"That's right, princess. Take it all," he urged, hips rolling beneath her.

Despite the rhythmic thrusts, his eyes never left hers. The

rest of the world fell away, leaving only Ryan and those striking blue eyes of his.

God, if she wasn't careful she could lose herself in them.

Chloe threw her head back and lifted her hips, pulling back until only the tip of his cock remained inside her. Then she slammed her hips back down, clenching him tight. The guttural sound that erupted from Ryan was music to her ears as she rocked her body, feeding on his excitement. She cupped her breasts, squeezing them as he watched, knowing the action would heighten his pleasure.

He rattled the cuffs again. "Put those beautiful tits in my mouth. Let me suck them for you."

She shook her head and gave him a wicked grin. "I have a better idea."

With false bravado, she slid one of her hands down her belly, coming to a rest at the place where their bodies joined.

"Fuck, yeah," he rasped, eyes wild. "Touch yourself while you're riding me."

With experienced fingers, she rubbed her swollen clit. Ryan's thrusts become even more insistent, lifting them both from the mattress as he pushed them toward oblivion. It didn't take long. Within seconds, shockwaves rocked Chloe, shattering her focus. Her body clenched tight around Ryan, drawing him over the precipice with her. And then they were falling together, entwined as one as they rode out the aftershocks, utterly spent.

12

RYAN

GET IT THE FUCK TOGETHER, asshole.

Ryan laced up his skates, doing breathing exercises to calm his nerves. It wasn't practice that had him sweating. It was the prospect of facing Bash. The tension in the locker room was so thick he was choking on it. They needed to squash the drama and focus on the game. Personal shit was a distraction, one the team couldn't afford if they wanted to move into first place.

Still, he could feel the eyes of his teammates on him, wondering how he'd react when Bash arrived. And as usual, Bash was late.

Hell, if he didn't show up soon, Ryan would be on the ice before he made an appearance. That was the last thing he wanted.

The drama needed to stay in the locker room and off the ice.

Head down, he knotted his laces, fully aware the sudden hush meant Bash had arrived.

Doing his best to play it cool, he turned to his locker and grabbed his gloves, busying himself with them as Bash dropped his bag across the aisle. The hair on the back of his neck stood on end. Everyone was watching him, no doubt wondering if he'd be able to restrain himself from putting a fist to Bash's nose. He grabbed his helmet, watching his teammate from the corner of his eye as he slipped into his compression shorts.

"What the fuck!" Bash shrieked, grabbing his balls and tearing the shorts off. "Who put fucking Icy Hot in my cup?"

Ryan laughed. So did the rest of the team. And like that, the tension dissipated.

They were a team after all. Nothing could tear them apart. He wouldn't allow it.

"You should be more careful about where you put your dick."

Bash eyed him warily. He wrapped a towel around himself and made his way across the aisle. "We cool?"

"Yeah, man. We're cool."

"I've missed you. Hell, the whole team has." Relief washed over his face as Bash shifted uncomfortably. "Glad you're back."

"Me, too. Looking forward to getting back on the ice."

"Dude. If you guys start making out, I'm gonna hurl," Jordy said, clapping Ryan on the back.

Everyone laughed again and Ryan put his fist up, doing the guy thing and giving Bash a fist bump. "Let's hit the ice."

While the other guys filed out of the locker room, he sent Chloe a quick text.

You were right. Icy Hot in the jock was priceless. You should have seen his face. Guys loved it.

No sooner did he push send than his phone rang and Chloe's name flashed across the screen.

"Hey, princess."

"What the fuck, Ryan!" she yelled, ignoring the pet name she hated more than him. "Have you seen Page Six? Not only did that scumbag pap sell them the pictures from the other night, somehow they got pics from the bodega."

"Slow down. What are you talking about?"

"Listen to this... Ryan Douglas and his new flame were *shopping together* when an armed robber entered the store. Our sources tell us the *couple* disarmed the assailant and held him until police arrived. According to the police report, Ryan's new love interest is none other than Chloe Jacobs, a Junior Associate at Pritchard, Bennett, and Associates. Could it be love? We think the story certainly has a Hollywood feel!"

Ryan snickered at the ridiculousness of the whole thing. Who he was fucking hardly qualified as news. "What's the big deal? Nobody reads that crap anyway."

"You're kidding, right?" she asked, her voice rising an octave. "This is New York City. Everyone reads that crap!"

"Who cares?" he asked, trying another angle

He'd hoped the photog had taken only his picture at the restaurant, but clearly it was wishful thinking. Much as he'd wanted to smash the guy's camera for the way he was eyeing Chloe, that sort of behavior only incited the paps further. What was done was done. Besides, in a day or two, *The Post* would be back to reporting on debutants and other inane bullshit.

They'd be old news.

"Who cares?" she shrieked. "Me! I care. I told you, I'm done with men. Especially athletes. Been there, done that, better off single. Hell, I'd rather die a spinster. No offense. Besides, it's not even true. We had sex. Last I checked, that didn't make us a couple."

Ryan scrubbed a hand over his face, unsure of how to respond.

She wasn't exactly wrong. They definitely weren't a couple.

No way in hell was he going down that road again.

Not after the way things with Kelsey had crashed and burned.

"My X feed is blowing up. Half of them congratulating me

for banging such a hottie, the other half swearing to beat my ass for snagging their fangirl crush."

"Come to the game with me tonight," he offered, the words pouring out before he could consider what he was asking.

"What? No way. Did you hit your head at practice?" she asked, disbelief coloring her words. "Did you even hear a word I said?"

"My head is fine. And I heard everything you said." He grinned, imaging her pissed off and flushed. How such a tiny woman could channel so much aggression was beyond his comprehension, but he was more than happy to help her find a physical outlet for it. "People will expect you to be there. And, more importantly, it will look good to your boss and get extra press for Garden of Dreams. You know what they say in PR. Any press is good press, as long as people are talking."

She muttered something unintelligible, a sure sign she was cussing like a drunk sailor.

"It'll be fun. We'll sit in the owner's suite with the other guys on injured reserve." He paused, giving her time to think it over before delivering the knockout punch. "And if you're a good girl, I'll take you home and fuck you so hard you won't give two shits about Page Six or online trolls."

The sharp intake of breath on the other end of the line was all the answer he needed. Unfortunately, his dick didn't get the message this was a future offer of pleasure, not one to be played out immediately. He bounced on his skates, adjusting his padding and loosening his suddenly too tight balls.

"Fine. But I'm only doing this for Garden of Dreams. What should I wear?"

13

———

CHLOE

RYAN CUT ACROSS THE CONCOURSE, making a beeline for the concierge area. Chloe stayed nipping at his heels—no small feat considering the five-inch stilettos she was wearing. Normally she loved large crowds, but after the feature on Page Six, she would happily retreat to the privacy of the suite and avoid the masses.

And the masses were pumped.

The Garden was pulsing with energy and everyone seemed to be caught up in it, even Ryan. The Rangers were facing the New Jersey Devils, and apparently it was a pretty big deal. At least that's what Wikipedia said.

She snickered.

Ryan would probably shit if he knew she'd had to Google the teams.

She glanced down at her dress. Had she chosen conservatively enough? The black wool felt Upper East Side to her, but what did she know about Lifestyles of the Rich and Richer? Only what she'd read on the internet. And while she didn't know crap about hockey, she knew anyone who had an owner's suite at The Garden probably fell into the latter category.

The last thing she wanted to do was embarrass herself tonight. Or Ryan.

Plus, she wasn't looking for an encore appearance on Page Six. The irony of it wasn't lost on her, considering the only reason she'd agreed to go to the stupid game with him was to garner press for Garden of Dreams and maybe do a little networking.

Stopping at the bank of elevators labeled CLUB LEVEL, Ryan turned, finding her eyes glued to his ass.

Busted. Yeah, that earned her a smirk and a full frontal of his unmatched hotness.

The man looked good in his uniform, but in a suit? He was hot as puck. And he knew it.

Adding insult to injury, he dragged a hand through his hair, brushing aside the strands that framed his angular face. He was worse than any woman, leaving the top button of his shirt open and teasing her with just a hint of the defined muscles that she knew shaped his chest and arms.

"Tease."

"After you, princess." He slipped an arm around her waist and guided her into one of the waiting elevator cars.

Despite the heavy fabric of her dress, she could feel warmth emanating from the open palm cupping her back. When his thumb made a lazy pass across her lower vertebrae, her body responded immediately. Such a simple thing, but it warmed her belly, lust pooling hot and heavy.

Molten even.

His touch had that effect. The man could take her from ho-hum to total eruption in a heartbeat. Like Maytag, he was built strong to last long.

Fuck. Rest. Repeat.

The elevator attendant smiled knowingly, igniting her cheeks.

Shit. One look and even he knew she didn't belong. That, or he knew she had a gutter brain.

Unable to decide which was worse, she stared at her reflection on the door, refusing further eye contact.

They rode up to the suite level in silence.

She wanted to grab Ryan's hand and assuage her nerves, but she didn't want to do anything that might attract unwanted attention. Behind closed doors she could fuck his brains out, do every filthy little thing her dirty mind could conceive of, but holding hands in public was off-limits.

Not that she was complaining. The sex was more than enough.

After they completed the obligatory introductions and hand shaking, they settled into their seats to watch the game. Ryan was totally invested in his team's play, leaning forward with his elbows on his knees, eyes tracking every movement on the ice. She watched quietly for a while, following the cheers of the others in the suite, but eventually it became painfully obvious she was going to need an actual explanation of the rules.

"All right," she said, poking Ryan in the ribs. "You're going to have to explain it to me because I don't have the first clue what's going on down there."

Incredulous didn't even begin to describe the look on his face when he finally wrenched his eyes from the ice, as if he couldn't fathom someone not being an expert on his life's passion. "Explain it? Explain what exactly?"

Might as well have some fun with it. Chloe waved her hand. "All of it."

He groaned. "Why don't you start by telling me what you know and I'll fill in the gaps?"

Oh, this was going to be good. She beamed at him. "All I got so far is a bunch of brutes slapping a Hostess Ding Dong around and trying to slip one past the goalie."

Judging by the look on his face and the crimson flush making its way down his neck to disappear into the collar of his shirt, it was entirely possible his head was going to explode.

And not in the good way.

"Are you fucking with me?" he asked, narrowing his eyes.

Chloe burst out laughing and patted his chest. "Little bit. But seriously, what the hell is offsides?"

To his credit, he explained the basics in under five minutes, giving her a much better idea of what the heck was going on and when to cheer. By the middle of the second period, she felt like a pro, screaming right along with everyone else when two of the players dropped their sticks and started slugging it out, tearing at one another's jerseys and throwing punches.

"Does that get you off, princess?" Ryan asked, leaning in close, invading her space and leaving only a sliver of air between them.

She glanced down at her hand, which seemed to have a mind of its own. It was the only explanation for why she was rubbing his inner thigh like a horny teenager, and in a room full of strangers no less. Before she could withdraw it, he grabbed her wrist, holding her in place just inches from his cock.

The place she would have unwittingly gone if he hadn't stopped her.

"I should have known." The corner of his mouth crept skyward in that irritatingly sexy way of his. Her pulse thundered, drowning out the sounds of the game, the crowd, and even rational thought. "Meet me in the bathroom."

For once she had no snarky reply, only a dry mouth and a shit-ton of nerves.

He couldn't be serious. No way was she going in there with him.

It was a bathroom for God's sake. *Eww*.

Then again, it was a bathroom, in a very public place, with a captive audience right outside. It was dirty, inappropriate, and damn if she didn't want it. *Bad*. Forget the Mile High Club, she wanted Ryan to bend her over the sink and make her scream.

A quick scan of the suite confirmed everyone was engrossed in the game.

Would they even notice their absence? Doubtful. And even if they did, they'd probably assume she'd gone for another drink.

She chugged her beer.

Yeah, it was definitely time for a refill.

14

RYAN

RYAN STROKED HIS COCK, praying Chloe wasn't about to leave him hanging. He was so fucking hard he'd probably lose it as soon as he slipped inside that tight little pussy of hers. Seeing the look in her eyes as she'd watched that fight, he'd known then and there they weren't going to make it back to her place.

The door clicked open.

Chloe slipped through and locked it behind her, looking decidedly sure of her decision. Wearing a plain black dress and minimal makeup, she'd done her best to appear conservative. Only there was no taming those wild curls of hers.

Like her personality, they were larger than life.

His eyes flicked to her feet.

Those shoes. Those fucking gold snakeskin heels. They'd been taunting him all night, silently begging him to unleash his most burning desires.

Well, the time had finally come.

He seized her hips and lifted her in the air, spinning her around and sitting her on the edge of the counter. Wedged between her knees, he gripped her ass and pulled her body flush to him. He scraped his teeth over her jaw, losing himself in her sweet scent. Then, twisting his fingers in her hair, he exposed her neck, continuing the rough exploration of her body.

She mewled with satisfaction.

"For the record, there's nothing conservative about these shoes." He spread her legs and stroked her left calf, massaging her taut muscles all the way down to the offending gold shoe.

"Yeah, well, I'm not really into boring." She wiggled her hips in a fruitless attempt to get closer. "What're you waiting for?"

"This is going to be fast and hard," he warned her, shoving her skirt up around her waist. "Think you can handle it?"

She raised a brow. "Can you?"

"Princess, I've been dying to feel you wrapped around my cock from the moment I last saw you."

"There's a condom in my purse," she said, handing him the little gold clutch that matched her shoes.

She went to work on his belt, dropping his pants in record time and taking his erection in hand, squeezing the base and rubbing her thumb over the head. When he was ready, he shoved her panties aside, revealing her smooth entrance. Chloe silently guided him in, wrapping her legs around his waist.

"Hold on to the counter," he ordered, planting a deep kiss on her lips before he drew back and thrust into her.

"Oh," she moaned, burying her face in his shoulder.

Christ she was wet. Which explained her willingness to follow his lead, having sex in a highly inappropriate place, consequences be damned.

He shoved the thought aside, pumping into her hard and fast as promised. Her body tightened around him, creating such an intense friction he knew he'd better work quickly to deliver his partner an O. Licking his thumb, he wedged his hand between their bodies and stroked her clit. She bit down on his shoulder. Apparently she was closer than he'd thought.

Good. They were coming together or not at all.

He tilted his hips, angling for the spot that would give her the most intense orgasm. Her back arched and he clamped his mouth down on hers, swallowing her cries of pleasure as his own orgasm shot through him, leaving little shudders of pleasure in its wake. Her body sagged against him, her head resting on his shoulder.

"We should go," she mumbled, not moving.

He lifted her head and kissed her, soft and languid this time. "We should do this again," he suggested, pulling out and discarding the condom.

"Yeah, like every week," she agreed, adjusting her underwear. She slid off the counter and pulled her dress down. "I'll bring the shoes, you bring the condom."

15

CHLOE

CHLOE SCANNED THE ALWAYS-CROWDED STARBUCKS, spotting Olivia at a small table wedged in the back corner. As usual, Liv was hard at work, head down and typing on her iPad. And Chloe was late.

The upside? Olivia had already grabbed her a calorie-heavy Pumpkin Spice Latte it would take an hour on the treadmill to burn off.

If she could find the time.

The work with Garden of Dreams was keeping her busy and just finding time for coffee had been a struggle.

Shimmying between tables, she made her way toward the back of the restaurant and dropped unceremoniously into the seat opposite her friend.

"You're late," Olivia said, tapping her screen a few more times before sliding the tablet into its case and looking up.

"And you're wearing the Crown-*freaking*-Jewels!" Chloe blurted out, unable to tear her eyes away from the obscenely large diamond on Olivia's left hand. "Sweetie, that thing's going to blind someone. And *oh-my-God!* You're engaged! Why didn't you tell me?"

She jumped up from the table and threw her arms around her best friend, giving her a tight squeeze. No one deserved happily-ever-after more than Liv, and she was thrilled her workaholic friend had found her Prince Charming.

"I wanted to tell you in person." Olivia scrunched up her nose. "Besides, last week you said you were too busy at work for coffee, remember? What is up with that anyway?"

Chloe winked. "That man of yours is running me ragged at work. But if I'd known you had such big news, I'd have found the time. Let me get a good look." Grabbing Olivia's hand, she brought the ring up for closer inspection. "It's beautiful. Seriously, Liv. I am so excited for you. Tell me everything."

The glazed eyes and blissful smile on Olivia's face as she relayed Cole's proposal at the Macy's Thanksgiving Day Parade spoke volumes about their relationship. In all her life Chloe couldn't remember ever seeing a woman so in love.

"It's so unfair." She gave her friend a playful smile. "You guys haven't even been together a year. I've spent the last four years relentlessly searching for Mr. Right and I'm still stone-cold single."

"Really?" Olivia tilted her head and pressed her lips into a flat line. "Not according to Page Six."

The groan was off her lips before she could stop it. "Not you, too."

"What's the deal with you and Ryan Douglas anyway?" Liv asked. The look of hope on her face was soul crushing. "Have you been keeping secrets from me?"

"Hardly. Things with Ryan are just..." She wrinkled her brow searching for the right word. Fuck-buddies seemed a little crass, especially for broad daylight at Starbucks. "Fun."

In the blink of any eye, Olivia's hope shifted to concern. "You? Just for fun?"

"We are not dating. We just hooked up a couple of times. It's no big deal. It just sort of happened." Chloe shrugged, a smile pulling at the corners of her mouth. "Once in the kitchen. Once in the owner's suite at MSG. Once—"

"I don't need details," Olivia said, raising her hand and cutting her off mid-sentence. "I just don't want to see you get hurt. A pro hockey player? Seems like the kind of guy who checks all of your 'no-go' boxes. Cocky. Narcissistic. Entitled," she finished, ticking them off on her fingers.

"I'm fine. Really," Chloe insisted, waving off any further discussion of the potential for future heartbreak. She didn't need a reminder that Ryan was a walking deal breaker or that nothing could ever happen between them. She was acutely aware of the situation. "Actually, I'm better than ever. Things at work are going well and for the first time in forever, my life is free of boy drama. Being single has never felt better. If I could keep my face off Page Six and the Blueshirt hockey blogs, I'd be a freaking rock star."

Olivia shook her head, her eyes dancing with laughter. "I never thought I'd see the day when Chloe Jacobs wanted less attention, not more."

"Tell me about it. Seriously, though?" she said, happy to have someone she could trust and confide in. It felt like ages since she and Liv had sat down for girl time. "I used to love reading the gossip magazines, but I swear I'm canceling all my subscriptions. I mean, surely people have better things to worry about than who I'm screwing? Or rather, who Ryan's screwing." Reaching into her bag, she pulled out a wrinkled copy of *The Post*. "And they can't even take a decent picture. Look how big and frizzy my hair is! Does it really look like that from the back?"

Olivia chuckled. "Your hair is fine."

Lady Gaga's *Telephone* blasted from Chloe's purse. She rolled her eyes. "Not again." Fishing the phone out of the bag, she confirmed what she already knew. Dave. Or, as she'd come think of him, Dave the Douche. He'd been blowing up her phone for days, and she was getting tired of dodging him. "Hang on," she told Olivia, holding up a finger. "Let me just see what he wants."

"Hello?"

"Hey, Chloe. How've you been?" he asked, doing his best to sound casual, although they hadn't spoken since their broken date.

Too bad the tremor in his voice gave him away. Talk about fifty shades of awkward.

"Never been better." Which was actually the truth, she realized, a smile curving her lips. "What do you want, Dave?"

"Listen, I'm sorry for canceling our date last week. Something came up." He paused. *Ha!* It didn't take a genius to figure out what had come up: a better prospect. "Anyway, so I was thinking maybe we could give it another try this weekend?"

Was he for real? No one could be that self-involved and arrogant. But apparently he was.

Her temper started to build, hot and angry, churning in her belly. Stupid asshole. He'd had the balls to dump her with a text message and now that he'd seen her face on Page Six, he wanted to give it another go? Did he really think she was that desperate and pathetic?

She'd eat glass before she'd date him again.

Or any guy like him—including Ryan.

With herculean self-control, she swallowed the angry rhetoric nanoseconds before it exploded from her mouth, earning her a lifetime ban from Starbucks. No way in hell was she giving up her Pumpkin Spice Lattes for Dave the Douche. The man needed a hefty dose of karma. And she was happy to oblige.

"Actually, I'm free Saturday night if you are."

"Really?" The man must've been smarter than he looked because he actually sounded surprised.

"Sure. Why don't we meet at Zero Sum at eight o' clock? We can grab a few drinks and see where the night takes us."

"Great. I'm really looking forward to it."

"Me, too," Chloe lied with only a twinge of guilt. "Gotta run, but I'll see you Saturday."

Olivia eyed her as she tucked the phone back in her bag. "Did you really just make a date with another man when you are banging that sexy hockey player?"

"Not one I plan on keeping." She snorted and sipped her latte. Sadly, Dave wasn't even the first ex to come crawling out of the woodwork. Just the most recent. Her phone had been ringing off the hook since the article in *The Post*, which was why she'd started moving all her exes onto the same ringtone. One that reminded her they weren't worth her time. The past was the past for a reason and she had no desire to look back. "Trust me, Dave is an enormous ass. I guarantee the only reason he called is because he saw Page Six. Last week I wasn't even worth a phone call." She rolled her eyes and tucked her hair behind her ear. "How ironic is it the guy I'm screwing for fun is the one making other guys take notice?"

16

RYAN

RYAN WATCHED his teammates as he strapped on his shin guards. He was so fucking tense he wanted to hurl. A scan of the circular locker room revealed he wasn't the only one battling elevated emotions.

It was his first game back, and while it was a regular season game, this wouldn't be just any faceoff. They were playing the Flyers, one of their top rivals and the team that had put him on IR.

Tensions were high and The Garden was sold out.

The crowd was expecting a hard-hitting game and they were going to get it tonight. There was no love lost between the teams, especially after the nasty injury to his calf. The fans would also be riding high and extra security had been brought it to manage the unruly crowd.

Hell, he couldn't wait to get back on the ice.

The rush of the game, the lights, the crowd—he hadn't realized how much he had missed it.

Hockey was a part of him. It was who he was. And he relished the opportunity to get back out there and show all the haters he could face the adversity and come back stronger than ever.

He wasn't a quitter, could never be one.

Despite Kelsey's parting shot as she walked out the door.

Ryan sucked in a deep breath and stretched his calf, rubbing the scar that stretched from the back of his knee down toward his ankle.

The past was the past. It was time to bury the pain and focus on the game.

As a captain, the weight of expectation fell heavy on his shoulders. His team was counting on him. Despite all the press, all the doubt, he knew they had his back. They always did. He felt confident and prepared, but that didn't mean things would go their way tonight.

They needed the win. Not just for the standings, but to confirm they were one team again, strong as ever. That was the whole reason he'd stayed upstate at the training center for the last week. To rebuild the team. Not that he didn't need the extra time with the coaches and trainers. He sure as hell did. And every bit of it was paying off.

Maybe he wasn't quite one hundred percent, but he was damn close.

Tonight that would have to be good enough.

The only downside to bunking at the training center was the fact that it was a testosterone fest. Which had done nothing to temper his thoughts of Chloe's lush little body. The sex was un-fucking-believable, and he'd jerked off more times than he cared to admit just thinking of her. The way she came alive when he touched her was a real turn-on.

Unlike some of his teammates, he hadn't been with many women, but he'd definitely never been with one as responsive as Chloe. The woman was an untapped frontier of sexual exploration. Not only was she open to it, she delighted in it.

Things with Chloe were totally different than they'd ever been with Kelsey.

Even in the beginning, things with his ex had felt like work. Had he booked the right restaurant? Worn the right shirt? Bought the right gift? Hell, Chloe was a breath of fresh air with her sarcastic little mouth and lack of expectations. Living in the here and now, just having fun in the moment, was exactly what he needed.

"Yo, Ry. What the fuck are you doing over there?" Jordy threw a balled-up sock at him. "Get your head in the game, man. Warm-up's in five minutes."

He glanced down, realizing he was far from game ready. Grabbing his jersey, he slipped it over his shoulder pads. Jordy was right. He needed to table all thoughts of sex and get his head in the fucking game.

After? Well, that was a different story.

17

CHLOE

CHLOE SHEPHERDED her rambunctious little charges from the Garden of Dreams to their seats, doing everything in her power to keep the kids moving in an orderly fashion. She'd been flattered when Becca, the Garden of Dreams liaison, had extended the invitation for her to join them at the game. Spending time with the kids was proving more fulfilling than she could have imagined, and it would give her an opportunity to see the crowd's reaction to the new Garden of Dreams campaign firsthand.

Her belly twisted in knots. The new spot was scheduled to run on the big screen right before the game. She was proud of the work they'd done, but it was impossible to predict how people would react.

For the kids' sake, she hoped positively and with open checkbooks.

Especially since there was a call to action inviting the crowd to text donations before the puck dropped.

Seeing Ryan's comeback game live was just an added bonus.

"Here's your seat, Elijah." Extricating herself from the hand of the little boy, whose death grip had cut off all circulation to her fingers fifteen minutes ago, she took the seat next to him.

The rest of the kids settled into empty seats between her and Becca, the group's other chaperone.

"Wow." Elijah's eyes grew wide as he surveyed the arena. "This is awesome, Miss Chloe."

"It is pretty awesome, isn't it?" she agreed, grinning.

She was anxious to see Ryan play. They hadn't seen one another since last weekend. He'd texted a few times, but he'd been busy with practice, and even though she missed the sex, her life remained drama free.

It was refreshing to say the least.

Would he even know she was here tonight?

Probably not. It was unlikely the players knew everything going on within the Rangers' organization or Garden of Dreams.

They had other priorities. Like the hunt for the Cup.

She grinned, pleased with her newly acquired hockey knowledge. Not that she'd ever admit it, but Ryan had opened her eyes to a sport she'd never really considered in the past. She'd be an expert in no time.

Of course, her interest was strictly professional.

Maybe she should have texted him and told him she'd be at the game. But it wasn't like they had a commitment or anything. Better to play it cool.

Chloe glanced at her watch and settled in to wait for the Garden of Dreams spot. It would be airing any minute.

Even if she hadn't been watching, she'd have known the second it came on.

The kids leaped from their seats, squealing with delight when their faces appeared on the big screen. She watched the video with a critical eye, finally admitting to herself it had turned out pretty damn great. Her shoulders dipped and she released a breath she hadn't realized she was holding. The video was just the right mix of depressing '*How do you sleep at night?*' followed by an upbeat '*You can make a difference!*' vibe.

Only a stone-cold bastard could look at those glowing little faces and not want to help.

At least, that's what she was counting on.

When the cameras panned their section, putting the kids on screen live, she waved graciously, reminding herself that any PR was good PR. Even if it was likely her presence would ignite a new round of speculation about her non-existent relationship with Ryan.

Chloe watched the crowd, very aware that sitting among the raucous fans was a completely different experience than being tucked away in a suite with the upper crust of society. And even though the crowd was wild tonight, screaming and chanting and stomping, she preferred it. They were going nuts waiting for Ryan and the other Rangers to take the ice.

Of course, she could do without some of the signs. Put it in MY five hole, Ryan!, I want my headboard to give you a concussion, Jordy! and Puck Me, Gabe! were among her least favorites.

Seriously?

When the lights dimmed signaling the players would be taking the ice, Chloe felt a flutter of panic in her belly. The Rangers were playing the Flyers. Was Ryan up to it?

Hockey was an incredibly physical game, and she knew he needed a win tonight to get his confidence back. And her stupid nerves were getting the best of her. Which was silly. Ryan was a pro. By his own proclamation he'd been skating as long as he'd been walking, so pretty much his whole life. He'd be fine.

Besides, what they had was just sex.

She didn't need to worry about him or his feelings or any of that other mushy stuff. The only thing she needed to worry about was showing the kids from Garden of Dreams they, too, could overcome adversity, right?

18

RYAN

RYAN WATCHED from the tunnel while the other Rangers skated onto the ice and lined up. He paused, dragging in a deep breath and filling his lungs to capacity with the frosty air. Sweat trickled down the back of his neck.

It's now or never.

"You've got this," he said, needing to hear the words spoken aloud.

Now sure as shit wasn't the time to fall apart. The team was counting on him.

Stuffing his fear down, he stepped onto the ice, his heart slamming against his rib cage. The spotlight found him immediately, sending the crowd into a thunderous applause. The guys tapped their sticks on the ice, leading the arena in a chant.

Douglas! Douglas! Douglas!

He was home, back on the ice where he belonged. Skating to the line, he took his place among his teammates and waved to the fans, grateful for their support and knowing he was lucky to have it. Now it was time to prove he deserved it.

The Garden pulsed with energy and he drank it in, fueling his enthusiasm.

When the doc had given him the news about his leg, he'd been so afraid he'd never have this opportunity again. But here was he was, three months later, game ready. With a little more time, he'd be back in top form.

He cut his eyes at the Flyers.

They were glaring daggers, but he didn't give a fuck. No one was going to intimidate him.

Not tonight, not ever.

When the anthem was done and it was time to face off at center ice, he was ready. The crowd ceased to exist. He blocked out their cheering, the loud music, and the excited lilt of the announcer's voice. Squatting low, he choked up on the stick, fully prepared to sweep the puck back to his defensemen and take control of the game.

The ref blew his whistle and dropped the puck.

His stick was on it the instant it hit the ice, winning the faceoff easily. Putting his shoulder into the opposing center, he pushed forward, skating down the ice and getting into position to receive the pass he knew was coming.

The Flyers were fast, but his guys were prepared.

His eyes darted across the ice. Jordy still had the puck.

Boom! He was checked into the boards, but not before passing to Bash, who was on the breakaway.

The Flyers defense tried to sweep the puck from him, but Bash flipped the puck to Ryan.

It skipped over the Flyers sticks and landed in front of Ryan, who received it easily, drawing back and taking the shot on goal. The puck whizzed through the air, heading for the goalie's right shoulder.

Come on.

The puck pinged off the crossbar and bounced in. The siren

blared and the crowd went ape shit, the roar reaching a deafening pitch.

Ryan pumped his fist and checked the scoreboard.

Thirteen seconds. A new personal best.

Crunch! His face met the Plexiglas above the boards. Hard.

The solid surface was unforgiving, splitting his lip and giving him a taste of his own blood.

The fuck. Checked from behind after a shot on goal? Dirty.

He turned around, fully prepared to take a swing at the asshole who'd delivered the hit.

Fighting wasn't exactly his thing, and he could count on one hand the number of fights he'd had, but this wasn't happening. Fuck forgive and forget.

Maybe he could overlook the injury to his leg as a freak accident, but this was deliberate.

Before he could respond, Bash was on the player who'd hit him.

Hozier. No surprise there. The guy had a reputation for playing dirty.

Bash's fist crunched against the other player's nose, unleashing a crimson tide, which ran down his face, staining his jersey. Hozier swung back, but Bash deflected the blow, taking it on the shoulder. He had Hozier by the jersey, pounding the shit out of him.

The linemen stayed back, waiting for an opportunity to pull the two swinging giants apart.

Finally, when it looked like Hozier couldn't take another punch, Bash dropped him on the ice. He gave Ryan a fist bump and headed for the box where he was sure to spend five for fighting. Hozier would be joining him for boarding, another major penalty, so at least the penalties would offset.

Although spontaneous, the fight had amped the crowd up even further.

They were going crazy.

Some considered Bash a goon, but the title did him a disservice.

While he was the team's undisputed enforcer at six-foot-four and two-twenty, he was also a skilled player. But mostly he was loyal, as he'd proven tonight, jumping in to defend his team and his captain despite everything that had transpired between them over the last few months.

Collecting Bash's gloves from the ice, he skated over to the sideline and handed them off.

Then he grabbed a water bottle and rinsed his mouth, spitting blood onto the ice. The busted lip stung, but it was probably nothing compared to Hozier's nose.

Or his ego, for that matter.

Ryan looked into the stands and spotted a tiny, pissed off brunette waving her fist and no doubt cussing like a trucker.

The kids beside her stared wide-eyed and slack-jawed.

Unable to suppress the smile that spread across his face, Ryan found himself grinning like a fool. Chloe hadn't mentioned she was coming to the game. Talk about a pleasant surprise.

His night was definitely looking up.

Their eyes met, and her cheeks got a telltale flush of embarrassment when he winked at her, acknowledging her presence. For someone who didn't give two shits about hockey a week ago, she was awfully invested in the game tonight.

19

CHLOE

"Who knew you had such a filthy mouth on you?" Becca teased, tipping her drink to Chloe in salute. "Don't worry. I don't think the kids could actually hear what you were saying over the noise of the crowd."

Chloe shrugged and sipped her beer, pretending she hadn't wanted to completely die of embarrassment when Ryan saw her screaming like a nut at the game. She'd slunk down in her seat, reminding herself that *it was just sex.*

There was zero reason for her to be so invested.

Zero.

So why had her heart been beating double time?

And why had her palms been all sweaty?

Maybe those were typical reactions to hockey violence.

That was probably it.

Whatever the cause, it wasn't exactly her finest hour. She'd vowed to keep her head down and her mouth shut for the rest of the game.

Which had proven easier said than done.

It was a fast-paced, hard-hitting sixty minutes. By the time the buzzer sounded, she was emotionally drained from the adrenaline rollercoaster. Thankfully, the Rangers had pulled it out, three to two.

When Becca had begged her to grab a beer after the game, it had been a no brainer.

Needing something to distract her mind and her libido from Ryan Douglas, she hadn't even argued when Becca insisted they cab it uptown, hell-bent on scoring a table at some trendy new club. It was the kind of place Chloe herself would have relished spending an evening not too long ago. The kind of place where she'd met Dave the Douche. She hardly needed a reminder of how well that had turned out.

Which meant it was time to think happy thoughts.

"What did you think of the Garden of Dreams spot?" she asked, swirling her beer.

Becca pressed her lips into a flat line, apparently weighing her response. "I'm no expert, but if it brought in that kind of money from just one showing, you've got a winner on your hands."

"Here's hoping," Chloe agreed, a warm glow spreading over her body. It was hard to remember the last time she'd been so proud of her work. When the GoD donations flashed on the big screen at the end of the game, she'd nearly gone into shock. She'd hoped the kids would melt a few hearts, but in her wildest dreams she hadn't expected donations to surpass six figures. It was surreal. "We'll be able to throw the kids one hell of a Christmas party!"

"Best ever!" Becca agreed, eyes scanning the crowded club.

"Looking for someone?" Chloe grinned. She'd know that look anywhere.

"No." The other woman replied automatically, redirecting her gaze to Chloe. The blood that rushed to her cheeks told a different story. "Just you, me, and a whole lot of Jose tonight." She signaled the waitress and ordered a round of shots.

Just as they were finishing their second round of beers, there was a commotion on the VIP balcony. Both Chloe and Becca turned to see security block off the lower landing as the Rangers' players lumbered up the stairs.

"Son-of-a-bitching-god-damn-mother-freaking-karma!" Chloe swore, throwing her hands in the air and rolling her eyes at the ceiling. "Can't I get a break for one night? In case you haven't noticed, I've been on my best behavior."

Becca avoided her gaze, shifting uncomfortably and looking guilty as sin.

Well, didn't that just figure? Her new friend had a mischievous streak.

"Did you know they were going to be here?" Chloe asked, resigned to her fate and scanning the club for the nearest exit.

Ryan hadn't seen her yet. Maybe she could still sneak out without looking like a stalker.

"I may have overheard the guys talking about it during sound bites yesterday." Becca flashed an evil grin. "What? We work side by side with them all the time and I still haven't gotten to meet Gabe Wright. He's only been to one event this season, and like the badass woman I am, I took one look at those dimples and choked! I couldn't think of a single thing to say." She groaned, looking utterly horrified by her own behavior

"Trust me. You're not missing anything. They're a bunch of self-involved asshats," Chloe assured her. She nodded at the security guard blocking access to the VIP area. They'd been in the club less than a minute, but already a horde of women had gathered, waiting to be invited up. "Besides, judging by the looks of it, you won't be meeting him tonight anyway."

The other woman sighed and crossed her arms over her chest, disappointment radiating from her every pore. "They can't all be that bad." She sniffed. "Look at all the charity work they do."

Since she had no reasonable counterargument, Chloe did the next best thing and ordered a conciliatory drink for Becca, figuring she owed the other woman at least one more round before calling it a night. It was a big club. She'd be gone before Ryan ever knew she was there.

Or not.

It wasn't long before she felt the telltale burn of Ryan's gaze on the back of her neck.

Doing her best to ignore him, she focused on the conversation with Becca, leaning toward the other woman and using every last drop of willpower to avoid looking up into that balcony.

Several women had been admitted, and the last thing she needed was to see one of them draped all over Ryan. Not that she cared what he did. After all, she knew his type, didn't she?

Too bad Becca's eyes kept shifting that direction.

When she couldn't take it any longer, Chloe excused herself and went in search of the bathroom.

She shimmied through the crowd, getting pushed around more than she would have liked in the pulsating club. Still, it was better than being a sitting duck under Ryan's demanding gaze.

In the bathroom, she splashed some cold water on her face and ordered herself to pull it together. Sure it had been a strange night, but it was almost over. She just had to hang in a little longer. Turning from the sink, she bumped into a woman who'd apparently missed the memo on personal space.

"So you're dating Ryan?"

It wasn't so much a question as an accusation.

She brought her eyes up slowly, taking in the lithe blonde who stood in front of her. Had to be Kelsey, the ex-girlfriend from hell, who Ryan had mentioned was now dating another player. And of course she was freaking gorgeous. Tall, thin, immaculately dressed.

Chloe gave herself a mental face palm.

It would be a lot easier to hold her ground if she actually felt confident.

But standing face-to-face with Ryan's supermodel ex? Yeah, confident was nowhere on the list of things she was feeling.

Kelsey crossed her arms over her chest, literally looking down at Chloe from the top of her to-die-for calf-hair Burberry pumps. "Let me give you a little friendly advice, you know, girlfriend to girlfriend. If you like the lifestyle, I suggest you move on."

"Excuse me?" What the hell was she even supposed to say to something like that? *Thanks for the tip, but I'm not a after his money. I'm just in it for the sex.*

"Tonight's game was a fluke. Ryan will never make a full recovery. He's never had to work hard for anything—girls, grades, hockey." She flipped her hair in that holier-than-thou way popular girls learned to do in middle school. "I'd know. We were together for six years. Trust me on this. Don't waste your time. When things get tough, he'll crack."

What a heartless bitch.

No way was this chick going to intimidate her. Or scare her off. Or whatever she was trying to do.

Besides, it wasn't like she and Ryan were an actual couple. Far from it.

Wouldn't nice girl etiquette say kill 'em with kindness?

Screw. That.

"Now let me give you a little friendly advice, you know, girlfriend to girlfriend." Chloe smirked and stepped around Kelsey, pulling the door open. "Don't believe everything you read in the papers, sweetie. You'll drive yourself crazy."

On that note, she marched back to the table, head held high, feeling light as air, ready to grab Becca and get the hell out of dodge. Only Becca had different plans, plans that apparently included heading up to the VIP section with the team.

"No way," Chloe said, shaking her head emphatically and silently cursing the fact that her night had gone from amazing to shit-tastic in the span of just a few minutes. This was Ryan's doing. She knew it right down to her ovaries, which were suddenly very alert. "No. Way. I'm sorry, but it's not happening."

"Oh, it's happening," Becca said with a wicked smile, grabbing Chloe's arm and dragging her toward the stairs. "They're celebrating and they invited us up for a drink. It would be rude not to accept, and I am not missing my chance to meet Gabe."

Chloe arched her brow. "You two are on a first name basis now?"

Becca squealed and pulled Chloe close, ignoring her sarcasm. "I can't believe I'm going to meet Gabe Wright."

Being dragged to a VIP party against her will? Not how she planned to spend her night, but if she was going, then she was going to make it worth her while.

One drink wouldn't kill her and no way was she going to let Ryan or Kelsey or anyone else manipulate her. It was time to turn the tables. Ryan wanted her to come upstairs for a drink and play nice?

She'd show him nice.

And she'd wrangle a little more holiday cheer for Garden of Dreams while she was at it.

20

RYAN

RYAN WATCHED in awe as Chloe threw back a shot of whiskey and chased it with her beer, shaking her wild mane of curls as if she could cast off the sting of the alcohol. Jordy and Chloe were proving to be fast friends, and the half-pint would be toe up in no time if she didn't slow down.

There was no way she could keep up with him.

Jordy had thrown down the gauntlet and she'd accepted with her usual bravado.

In fact, if he didn't know better, he'd have thought she purposely goaded Jordy into challenging her.

Chloe slammed her glass down on the table, a triumphant grin on her face. The group of players that circled them cheered, encouraging her to do another shot. He gritted his teeth, hoping like hell she'd pass.

Trying to talk sense into her had been pointless.

In typical Chloe fashion, his argument had fallen on deaf ears. Or more likely, she'd done it to spite him, proving she would do whatever the hell she wanted whether he approved or not. Honestly, it didn't surprise him at all.

What did surprise him was how grossly the guys had underestimated her.

Apparently she hadn't been kidding when she said she could drink them under the table, and the guys were paying the price for it now. By his count, she'd scored two game jerseys, an appearance for the Christmas party, and a pair of club seats to the New Year's Eve game, all of which would benefit Garden of Dreams.

Jordy pushed another shot across the table.

Much to his relief, Chloe shook her head, signaling she was done with whiskey.

"Nice doing business with you boys, but I got what I came for. I'm going to dance." She sat her beer on the table and high-fived her friend, the two of them celebrating Chloe's hustle.

Turning from the table, she crashed into Ryan in the tight space.

His arms went around her protectively, preventing her from stumbling. Her body curled into him, her breasts pressed to his chest. And damn if he didn't want to hold onto her all night.

"Move aside, wallflower." She gave a throaty laugh and patted him on the arm, her dark eyes shining with life. "The dance floor is calling my name."

"You're going to go dance by yourself?" That sounded like the worst idea ever. She probably couldn't even walk straight, let alone dance.

"Why shouldn't I?" she asked, grinding her hips against his in a circular motion. On second thought, she seemed to have perfect control of her body. And his, too. His balls tightened in response to the feel of her soft curves against him. If she was trying to tempt him, she was definitely going about it the right way. "Won't be the first time."

"I wouldn't go too far if I were you," cautioned Jordy. He

wiggled his eyebrows suggestively. "The minute you turn your back, the puck bunnies will descend."

"What the hell is a puck bunny?" Chloe turned to Ryan expectantly.

No way was he going there. Shaking his head, he took a pull on his beer. "Don't look at me. Jordy brought it up, let him explain it."

"A puck bunny is a woman who likes to fuck hockey players," Jordy explained, completely matter-of-fact. "Single. Engaged. Married. With kids. They don't care. They just like to puck."

Chloe's eyes ricocheted from Jordy to Ryan and back again. She burst out laughing. "You're hilarious, Jordy."

"Who's joking?"

"Well, Ryan's a grown man and he can do what he wants. Despite that nonsense on Page Six, we're not a thing," she whispered. With the loud bass pumping through the speakers, it was more like a yell. Half the club probably heard her. "We're just...*friends*. Hell, we don't even like each other most of the time."

Jordy quirked a brow at Ryan as Chloe sauntered to the dance floor without a backward glance.

He shrugged. What could he say? The woman had spoken, making it perfectly clear what they were and what they were not. He knew the deal. It really didn't matter what anyone else thought, even if it did bruise his pride just a little to hear her say it so casually.

Chloe squeezed through the crowd, joining the hundreds of other pulsating bodies on the dance floor.

Curious, he watched as she closed her eyes and began to move her body in time with the music. It was like she absorbed the beat, her small frame twisting and writhing in ways that had his cock twitching in anticipation. She raised her arms over her head, extending her body into one sexy, long line. Shaking her ass, Chloe eased her body toward the floor. Her moves were slow and seductive, knees parted just enough to hint at what lay beneath the short skirt.

The reminder nearly pushed him over the edge.

There was nothing—*nothing*—he wanted more than to bury himself between those soft thighs. He would lick that sweet pussy of hers until she was thrashing against his mouth, back bowed, screaming his name with abandon.

Totally absorbed in the music, she seemed unaware of Ryan's gaze, or any of the other men watching her alluring dance. His gut twisted. He really didn't like the way they were watching her, eyes raking over her body, shit-eating grins plastered on their faces. Especially the guy in the silky purple shirt who seemed to be inching closer to her, preparing to make a move, like he thought he had a chance.

Taking a pull on his beer, he reminded himself Chloe was an adult. She was perfectly capable of taking care of herself. Hell, it was her mantra, and she'd reminded him no less than a dozen times.

Besides, he had no claim on her. Nor did he want one.

A hand clapped him on the back, and he turned to see Miller at his side.

The kid had just been traded a few months ago. He seemed nice enough, but he was still finding his place on the team. Tonight he reeked of alcohol, suggesting he'd had a few too many drinks.

Miller grinned up at him like they were old friends. "See you traded in the supermodel for a spinner."

Something dark and ugly rolled through him, and for the second time that night, he had the urge to put his fist through another man's face.

He gripped the edge of the table, keeping his hands steady.

The kid was lit. Probably didn't even know what he was

saying. Despite the baser urges insisting he defend his woman, he needed to respond as Miller's captain, not Chloe's lover.

That didn't mean he couldn't put the kid in his damn place.

"You've had too much to drink, Miller. Why don't you go home and sleep it off before you start something you can't finish?" He cut his eyes at the younger man. "And the next time I see you out, show a little fucking respect."

Without another word, Miller vanished into the crowd.

Ryan returned his attention to Chloe.

Purple shirt was within striking distance now. So close he could probably smell the sweet lure of her perfume mixed with the musky scent of the crowd. The way his eyes were fixed on her ass, there was no doubt he'd be rubbing his greasy body against her any minute, assuming that she was alone and looking for company.

No fucking way that was going to happen. The guy was about to find out just how wrong he was.

21

CHLOE

THE STRONG, steady beat of the music washed over Chloe, the seductive notes circling her like a lover's embrace, sweeping away coherent thought. On the dance floor she didn't have to think or even care. She could just be. There were no exes, no paps, and no pressure. It felt glorious to let go and lose herself in the vibrations of the music, melding into the rhythmic motions of the crowd.

A hand latched onto her waist. She twisted around, slipping free of the unwanted contact.

When it returned seconds later, skating over her midsection, it was clear a more direct approach would be required. Fixing a smile on her face, she turned to the guy with the roving hands. He wasn't unattractive and clearly had confidence to spare, judging by the purple satin shirt he wore.

Still, she wasn't interested.

"I prefer to dance alone." She removed his hand, hoping he'd get the message.

"Really?" he asked, his mouth twisting into a less than sincere smile. "Because it sure as hell looked like you were in the mood for some company."

"Back off," she warned, crossing her arms over her chest and staring pointedly at his junk. "Unless you want to spend the rest of the night speaking soprano?"

He studied her, no doubt wondering if she was serious, before raking a hand through his hair and taking off in search of new prey.

Chloe returned to her dance, letting her eyes drift shut as the pulsating crowd swallowed her once again. She relished the anonymity the club afforded. There was nowhere else could she be this free.

She sensed Ryan's presence before he touched her, his fingertips brushing the swell of her hip.

Testing. Teasing. *Tempting.*

Her eyes shot open.

And there he stood, a fantasy come to life, undressing her with those crystalline eyes. His long hair framed his face in that irritatingly sexy *I'm-hot-without-even-trying* look it would take her hours of styling and two tons of product to achieve. But when he stared at her like she was the only woman in the club?

She couldn't even pretend to be annoyed.

A new kind of warmth spread through her already heated body, fanning out from the spot where his fingers stroked her bare skin, blazing a trail toward her center. The man was intense, she'd give him that.

Desire coiled low in her belly.

Wrapping a powerful arm around her lower back, he claimed her. Their bodies crashed together, forcing the air from her lungs, but Ryan remained frozen, awkwardly immobile in the fluid crowd. Apparently he wasn't much of a dancer, so why the hell was he on the dance floor?

"What are you doing?" she demanded

"I could ask you the same thing," he returned, cutting his eyes at the dude she'd just chased off. "Who's your friend?"

"Jealous?" She didn't believe it for a second, but it seemed like a natural question. Why else would he have abandoned the comfort and security of the VIP section?

"Just wanted to make sure you didn't get into trouble," he replied, dodging her question.

Typical.

"Well, as you can see, I'm perfectly fine." She lifted her chin and pressed her hands to his chest, pushing him back and giving herself just enough room to maneuver. "And as I'm sure you heard, I'm not looking for a dance partner."

"Hate to break it to you, princess, but it looks like you found one all the same."

"Who? You?" she asked, not bothering to hide her disbelief as she took in his rigid stance. "Think you can keep up?"

"Can you?" he asked, no doubt knowing her stupid pride wouldn't let her walk away from a challenge.

Channeling her inner sex-kitten, she spun around, raking a hand through her hair as she brought her backside to his pelvis. She glanced over her shoulder and winked at him, rotating her hips and rubbing his cock with her barely covered ass. The growl that rumbled from his lips only solidified her resolve.

Forging ahead, she tipped her head and slid down the front of his body, dragging her back over his growing erection. The feel of his hardened cock gliding up her body was sinfully delicious, like a too rich dessert that would never be conquered. That was okay. She fully intended to push the limits of decency if that's what it took to make him back down.

Did he have any idea how erotic and sexy a simple dance could be?

Ever so slowly, she rose to her full height, skimming her palms over the soft fabric of his dress pants. The sculpted muscles that lay beneath called to her, a reminder of the thousands of hours he'd spent on the ice. Unfortunately, being a damn near perfect physical specimen wasn't a guarantee of rhythm. He remained stiff, unable or unwilling to succumb to the pulse of the music, completely separate from the beat driving Chloe's every move. The only change was the cadence of his breath on her ear.

She reached back over her shoulder and tangled her fingers in his hair, caressing his cheek and neck as she continued the rhythmic assault, letting the music rock her body without a care in the world.

That's all it took for Ryan's restraint to crack.

He gripped her hips, fingers digging into the flesh with unchecked hunger. Their bodies began to move in unison, like they'd done this hypnotic dance a thousand times before. The friction his thigh created as it rubbed against hers? It was bordering on orgasmic.

Chloe closed her eyes, reveling in his touch.

"Open your eyes." Ryan tipped her chin toward him with rough hands. It was a command, not a request. "You're going to keep your eyes open and look at me while we are dancing. And tonight when I take you back to my place? You're going to keep them open while I'm fucking you—first with my tongue, then my dick— so you can see just how much I enjoy pleasuring that sweet little body of yours."

Her mouth went dry. What could she possibly say to that? Yes, please? Two O's sounds great?

"And I'm going to watch you the whole time. Do you know why I'm going to do that, princess?"

She shook her head. As long as he was giving out orgasms, she didn't care why.

"I'm going to watch you so I can memorize the look on your face when I make you come. That look?" He rubbed his thumb across her bottom lip, leaning down and closing the distance between them. "It's going to get me through the next road series.

I'm going to go back to my hotel every night and remember what it's like to bury myself between your thighs, while I stroke one off."

"Wanna get out of here?" she asked, suddenly less interested in dancing and more interesting in getting naked.

Grabbing her hand, he led her back to the table where the others were still whooping it up.

Jordy's shot glass collection had grown considerably while they were gone. It was a wonder the dude was still standing. Then again, like Ryan, he was a giant so he could probably drink a whole damn bottle and still walk the line.

She said good night to Becca, checking to ensure her friend had a safe escort home.

Once again, she thanked the guys for their generous donations to Garden of Dreams and congratulated them on their victory over the Flyers. Jordy wrapped her in the mother of all bear hugs, nearly crushing her lungs. Then and there she made a mental note to never accept a drinking challenge from a professional athlete again, even if he did need to be knocked down a few pegs. Before he let go, he whispered a warning in her ear. "I've never seen Ryan dance—*ever*. Not even with Kelsey."

Fuck. She followed his gaze, confirming what she already knew.

Kelsey was sitting on Bash's lap, giving her a good old-fashioned death glare, which meant she'd probably be even more pissed off when she saw them leave together.

Talk about kicking the hornet's nest. "Looks like puck bunnies are the least of my worries."

22

CHLOE

Chloe stood at the door to Ryan's apartment, nerves tugging at her belly. Which was stupid. She and Ryan had hooked up lots of times. And thanks to Page Six, the whole world knew it.

What difference did it make where they did it?

His place was as good a place as any. No big deal. She couldn't very well expect him to come to her tiny apartment every time, could she?

Especially after his last visit.

She grinned. He was probably afraid she'd cuff him to the bed, *Misery* style, and never let him go.

The sex really was *that* freaking amazing.

Ryan opened the door and stepped aside so Chloe could pass by.

The second he closed the door to the apartment, her mouth was on him, devouring his lips with unrestrained passion. He must have liked it because that naughty tongue of his was doing dangerous things as he thrust it in her mouth, peppering her with little nips from his teeth. His cock responded to her immediately, pressing against the soft denim of his jeans. She gripped his front pockets and gave a tug, pulling his hips tight against her belly.

He swallowed a groan.

What the hell had come over her? It was like she'd thrown all her inhibitions out the window, acting on impulse alone. First the game, now this?

On second thought, as long as he kept those punishing kisses coming, she didn't care if she'd jumped feet first into the *Twilight Zone*. The feel of his erection pressed to her stomach had her body firing on all cylinders. It felt damn good.

Right up until Ryan pulled away, taking those addictive lips with him.

"Hey!" Chloe protested.

Pressing a finger to her lips, Ryan silenced her. "My house. My rules." To emphasize his point, he ducked down and wrapped his arms behind her knees, hoisting her over his shoulder. Chloe giggled. "Princess, there's nothing funny about what I'm going to do to you tonight. I meant what I said back at the club. You are going to watch every lick and thrust so you can remember who it is that makes you come so hard."

"Less talk, more action," Chloe quipped, her sarcasm earning her a swat on the ass.

Ryan's hand cracked against her backside, echoing through the silent apartment. It stung, but it was nothing compared to the ache she felt when he reached under her skirt to massage her bottom, his fingers toying with the edge of her underwear, skating oh-so-close to her aching center without actually making contact.

Damn. She needed to feel him inside her. Right-*freaking-*now.

Wiggling her bottom, she tried angling her body for sweet relief.

No such luck.

Ryan withdrew his hand, wrenching a tortured sob from her lips.

This was clearly another test of wills, and he was hell-bent on punishing her. He'd proven he could dish it out, but could he take it?

Pausing at the end of the hall, he flipped on the bedroom light. Then he dropped his shoulder, his hands skating over the curves of her body. A shiver ran straight up her spine as he lowered her to the floor. Her feet landed on a plush white rug that would have turned ten shades of filthy in her own apartment.

She scanned the room, taking in the masculine decor that was all Ryan.

The slate gray walls were a stark contrast to the white linens. And that bed. It was a monster.

Of course, Ryan was a giant, so that part kind of made sense.

Which reminded her, it was time to take back the control she'd had at the club.

Giving herself some breathing room, she strutted across the room, dragging a finger along the edge of the dresser as she passed. She wiggled her ass for good measure, knowing it would drive him wild, reminding him of their earlier dance. When she reached the bed, she kicked off her heels. First the right one. Then the left. She climbed up on the bed, remaining on her hands and knees, shamelessly flashing Ryan her red thong in the process. Twisting around, she blew him a kiss over her left shoulder.

That was all it took. He was on her in an instant. Grabbing her around the waist, he flipped her over and pinned her to the bed, the soft down comforter surrounding her as his massive weight pressed down from above.

"You are a very naughty girl," he said, toying with her hair.

"So I've been told. What are you going to do about it?"

"Princess, I am going to punish you all night long." He lowered his mouth to hers and kissed her slow and deep, drawing her back off the bed. She circled her hips, pushing them against his hardened cock. Once. Twice. She moaned, loving the feel of him between her thighs. "And you're going to enjoy every second of it."

Ryan pushed up off the bed and dropped to the floor. Pulling her hips to the edge of the bed, he settled between her knees. Chloe's legs shook with anticipation.

There was a very real possibility she'd be on the floor with him before he was done.

Ryan leaned close, licking her inner thigh with a slow, lazy scrape of his tongue. He moved north, kissing his way to the V between her legs. Blistering heat tore through her body as he licked her, sucking hard on her clit through the lace that separated their bodies.

"Take them off," she begged, desperate to feel his mouth on her. "Please take them off."

"When I take these tiny little panties off, I'm going to fuck you with my tongue," he said, pulling them down to her knees and pausing. "And you're going to watch me. Understand?"

She moaned again, unable to help herself.

Her head rolled to the side as she twisted her fingers in the comforter. When he put his tongue on her again, she was going to come. No doubt about it.

"Look at me," he ordered, biting the inside of her thigh as he dragged the thong down over her feet. Chloe sat up, locking her gaze on him, legs quaking with anticipation. "That's my girl."

Ryan's eyes never left hers as he spread her legs wide and devoured her. The moment his tongue touched her, she spiraled toward release, her body clenching tight as he circled her clit, working her to the brink of madness. Staring straight into his eyes, she called out his name, her body rocked by the intensity of her orgasm.

Laying boneless in his bed with her feet dangling over the side, she wondered if there was another orgasm in her immediate future. After all, back at the club he'd promised her two good ones.

It didn't take long to get her answer.

Ryan stripped off his T-shirt and jeans, standing before her naked as the day he was born, and she knew that sinful body of his would send her flying again.

He moved to the nightstand and retrieved a condom from the drawer.

Figuring she might as well look her fill while he had his back turned, Chloe rolled onto her side and admired his ass. She couldn't remember ever seeing it bare before, and it wasn't the kind of thing she was likely to forget.

Hell, if she had that ass, she'd run around commando, too.

"Admiring the view?" he asked, turning to face her, the grin on his face confirming he already knew the answer.

"Something like that," she said, climbing to her knees and meeting him at the edge of the bed.

She ran her hands over the smooth muscles of his stomach, relishing the way they rippled under her touch. Was he ticklish? She made a mental note to test the theory later, when it wouldn't jeopardize a perfectly good orgasm.

Stroking the head of his penis, she pulled him close and fused her mouth to his. She closed her eyes, losing herself in the kiss as his lips moved hungrily over hers. The space between them evaporated and once again, Ryan lifted her from the bed, lying her down on her back, his body positioned above her. Chloe nibbled his bottom lip, enjoying the lingering taste of spearmint on his breath.

She whimpered when he pulled away.

"Open your eyes."

"Didn't we already play this game?" she teased, jutting out her bottom lip.

He swooped down and bit it, tugging gently. As he sucked on her lip, Chloe forgot all about games, winners, and losers. She only had one thing in mind, and Ryan would deliver.

When he pushed into her, filling her completely, she cried out, knowing the feeling of euphoria would quickly grow to a mind-blowing crescendo. His eyes remained fixed on hers as he slowly withdrew and sank back into her, burying himself to the hilt. Each move was slower than the last—deliberately, excruciatingly slow.

Her skin was too tight, her temperature too hot. Every nerve in her body tingled with pleasure as their bodies joined, blurring the line between them. It was intense and exquisite and reality altering.

She never wanted it to end.

Staring into his eyes as he pleasured her body? Knowing he was watching every moan, whimper, and sob? Each arch of her back, twist of her head, bite of her lip?

It was sexy as hell. Erotic even.

Unable to take the slow glide any longer, Chloe rocked her hips, meeting him halfway.

Ryan groaned, pressing his forehead to hers. It was all the encouragement he needed.

Holding her tight, his fingers dug into her back as he pumped into her, their hips crashing together. Wrapping her legs around him, she gave herself over to the pleasure he offered. Need ripped through her body, seeking release for the tension that had coiled deep in her belly. Two more quick thrusts and her body shattered to pieces, clenching him tight and savoring the afterglow of amazing sex.

23

RYAN

RYAN TOYED with Chloe's curls, trying to decide the best way to wake her. His gut told him she wasn't a morning person. It also told him he was starving and there was nothing to eat in his cabinets except a few slices of bread.

Bread coated with a questionable green fuzz.

So, yeah, he was going to take his chances.

His stomach growled. *Again.*

Chloe's eyelids fluttered. "What time is it?" she grumbled, stretching and arching her back.

The woman had wicked sex hair, but he wasn't about to point it out. The look suited her just fine, and he was more than happy about his role in helping her achieve it.

"Almost nine." He leaned down and kissed her, loving the way she responded immediately, rising up to meet him, crushing her soft lips to his. "You want to grab breakfast?"

Pulling herself into an upright position, she glanced at her clothes, which he'd folded and laid across the foot of the bed. "Probably not a good idea."

"Why not?" He rubbed her knee absently. "You have to be hungry after last night."

"Hungry? Yes. Walk of shame? Not so much." She gave him a wry grin and pointed. "There is nothing about that shirt that is appropriate for nine a.m."

"Easy fix," he assured her. "My sisters are always forgetting stuff when they visit. I'll bet there's something that would fit you in the guest room. Get dressed. I'll go check."

Thirty minutes later he was ushering Chloe through the line at his favorite café, after finding her a turquoise shirt one of his sisters had left behind.

"You're really going to eat all of that?" she asked with a disbelieving stare as the cashier bagged his order.

He chuckled and paid for their food. "Skating burns a lot of calories. And I've always had a good metabolism."

"If I ate like a garbage disposal, I'd look like the Pillsbury Doughboy." She sighed and sipped her giant coffee. "So where are we going anyway?"

"It's a surprise," he said, slinging an arm across her shoulders and steering her out into the crisp December air. "I want to show you one of my favorite places in the city."

They stopped at The Garden, knocking on one of the service doors around back.

"You know, if you wanted to have sex, we could've skipped the cold and just stayed at your place," she quipped, gripping her cup with two hands. Steam escaped out the top, mingling with her frosty breath.

"Cute, but we're not here for sex."

The door opened and one of the security guards waved them in. "Cold one today," he said, closing the door behind them.

"Thanks, Joe." Ryan turned to Chloe. "This is my friend Chloe. I'm just going to give her a quick tour and then we'll be out of your hair."

"No problem, man. Take your time. Nothing going on this morning."

Sunday mornings at The Garden were usually pretty quiet, unless the Knicks were playing at home. It was Ryan's favorite time to visit. No crowds, no pressure, no responsibility. He could just soak up the silence and think. *Alone.*

In fact, this was the first time he'd brought anyone with him, he realized.

Not once had he brought Kelsey. It wouldn't have interested her. She'd never missed a game, and was always there for a public show of support, but hanging out at the rink on a quiet Sunday morning?

Not likely.

Trying not to think too hard about why he'd brought Chloe, he led her to the rink, choosing seats at center ice, where they ate in silence. He could feel her gaze on him, but it wasn't awkward or uncomfortable. If anything, it felt curious. Not surprising—after all, she had to be wondering why he'd brought her.

Hell, he wasn't quite sure himself.

Balling up the wrapper from his sandwich, he stuffed it back in the bag and finished off his orange juice.

"Playing for the Rangers has been a dream of mine for as long as I can remember." He leaned back in his seat and ran a hand through his hair, pushing it back from his face. How many times had he uttered that phrase? To reporters, fans, other players. It wasn't personal, but sitting in the quiet arena with Chloe, it felt that way. "My old man is a diehard fan. I grew up watching the Blueshirts. When I was eight years old, Mark Messier led the team to their first cup in over fifty years. I remember it like it was yesterday." He pointed to the rafters where red, white, and blue banners bearing the name and number of former players hung. "They retired his number in 2006."

"That's incredible." She dropped her hand on his, infusing it with warmth. "Most kids change their dreams a hundred times before they reach adulthood. And very few actually get to live them. You must've worked really hard to get where you are today."

He shrugged, embarrassed by her assumption. "When I was a kid, my parents brought me to New York to see the Rangers play. At the time, I thought it was the coolest thing ever." He shook his head, remembering how excited he'd been. "Even better than Disney World. I made sure we were waiting at the doors when they opened. I was on the edge of my seat trying to absorb every little detail of The Garden. My dad said to me, 'Ryan, if you work hard, you can make it. I know you've got the talent, son.' Even now his words are the one thing that stands out above the rest."

She grinned, her whole face lighting up. "Looks like you proved him right."

"I was really lucky." That part was true. He never would have made it otherwise. Even Kelsey, the one person he thought would always be in his corner, had seen it. "My parents were really supportive. Hell, they believed in me when no one else did."

She arched her brow and pursed her lips. "It can't all be luck. Give yourself some credit."

"I guess. I just don't want to let them down. When I got hurt, a lot of people said I'd never recover. Not my parents though. They said, get your ass back out there and prove them wrong."

"They sound like my kind of people."

"Are you kidding? They'd love you." He realized his mistake too late.

Chloe would never meet his parents. That wasn't what they were about.

Suddenly, he was at a loss for words. The silence that hung between them was beyond awkward. Painful, that's how he'd describe it.

Chloe stared at the ice. "Do you come here often to clear your head?"

"When I can," he admitted, impressed she'd made the connection. "Close your eyes."

She shot him a warning look, but complied, tipping her head back.

"Take a deep breath. Smell the ice. Feel the cold in your lungs. Now imagine yourself flying across the ice. The rush of adrenaline that comes with it." He closed his eyes, taking her hand in his. Despite all the intimate moments they'd shared, he was hyperaware of her presence next to him. Maybe it had been stupid to bring her here, but he couldn't turn back now. "Once it gets in your bones, you can never get it out. There's nothing like it in the world. I love the game."

Chloe sat up and turned to him, their knees bumping in the process.

"This is your place." She looked around, as if seeing it for the first time through his eyes. "The one place where everything makes sense."

He narrowed his eyes. How the hell had she managed to see it and articulate it so clearly, when he hadn't even known it himself until just a few months ago?

"You're a little too perceptive, you know that?" He squeezed her hand, seeking a lifeline as the words he'd never spoken aloud poured from his mouth. "Getting injured opened my eyes to the very real prospect of being traded. Or worse, permanently sidelined. Sitting around in that hospital room, I realized I had nothing without the game. No one gives a damn about Ryan Douglas the Sci-Fi geek with quick hands from Minnesota. They want Ryan Douglas, Captain of the New York Rangers and the NHL's hottest center. Ryan Douglas is nothing without the game. Without the fans, the fame, the money. *I* am nothing without the game."

And it scared the shit out of him.

24

CHLOE

CHLOE'S HEART faltered at Ryan's confession. Why had he told her those things? She hadn't asked, and she certainly hadn't expected him to spill his guts to her. Seeing Ryan as something other than the pompous, self-centered, pretentious jerk she'd met that first night at the bodega? It was too dangerous.

If she made the mistake of seeing him as anything else she might go and do something stupid like fall for him.

And she knew exactly where that road led.

Heartbreak Hotel.

Still, he was hurting and it wasn't in her nature to sit idly by while others were in pain. And somewhere along the way, she'd at least come to think of Ryan as a friend.

An annoyingly sexy friend, but a friend nonetheless.

Crawling into his lap, she twisted her body so they were face to face. His eyes were hard, like the ice he loved so much.

"I'm sure there are some scumbag freeloaders in your life who're happy to bask in your fame and fortune, but you know what?" she asked, stroking his cheek, desperate to soften those eyes. "When you're ready to cut them loose, you'll be stronger for it, and they'll help you appreciate the people who really matter. Your family, your friends, they'll be there for you no matter what. They love you for you, Ryan. Star Wars references and all."

He studied her, his face deadly serious.

"Are you making fun of me now?" he finally asked, a playful glint in his eye. "That's a dangerous game, one you are not equipped to win."

Before she could move, he was tickling her sides and she was squealing like a toddler, doing everything she could to wriggle from his iron grip. It was useless. She howled with laughter, begging for mercy.

When he finally stopped, she gasped to catch her breath.

"What about you?" he asked, dragging a gentle hand down her cheek and following the long line of her neck. Ryan's touch left a blaze of heat in its wake, stoking the always smoldering desire he evoked in her without even trying. "You're not like the others. Why is that? What are you so afraid of that you've sworn off men and settled for...whatever this is?"

Damn. She'd walked right into that one, hadn't she?

Maybe she should lie. It would be a hell of a lot less painful than admitting the truth.

But no, he'd been straight with her, and he deserved her honesty in return, no matter how uncomfortable it might be.

"I'm not afraid," she said, lifting her chin. "I'm exhausted. I've kissed my fair share of frogs, and all I got for my trouble was slimy lips. Hell, the last time I thought I found Prince Charming, he upgraded to a blond model who was a better fit for his image. She got the heirloom diamond; I got the curb."

"I'm sorry," he said, rubbing her arm and looking at her with such pity that anger bubbled up from her belly.

The last thing she wanted was pity. Especially from him.

"It was a long time ago." She shrugged, striving for indifference and tamping down the emotions that threatened to burst forth. He was worried about being traded? She could relate. She was tired of being traded. "Happily ever after is a fairytale that's not meant for me. Some women get it, some don't. I've got a great career, wonderful friends, and my very own sex god on speed dial. It's more than enough," she finished, wishing like hell she believed her own words.

25

CHLOE

Tucking her legs beneath her, Chloe settled into the couch with a glass of wine and her laptop. The game would be on in a few minutes, and she fully intended to get a glimpse of Ryan's sexy face while she worked. The Rangers were wrapping up a road series and she hadn't seen him in nearly a week.

Five days to be exact. Five long, frustrating, sex-free days.

Not that she was counting or anything.

Which just proved the time apart was probably good. It would keep her from becoming a sex-addled fool, something that was a very real risk with Ryan. At least she was putting her temporary celibacy to good use, keeping her promise to do something meaningful that had nothing to do with men or fairytales.

Although her job description technically ended at PR and Marketing for Garden of Dreams, the children at the foundation were impossible to let go. The more she got to know them, the more she wanted to help. When the opportunity to volunteer for their Christmas party presented itself, she jumped on it.

Plus, she could ensure the event got tons of PR, which meant more donations.

She'd even arranged an auction for the high-ticket items she'd hustled from the players. It was shaping up to be her very own hat trick.

Jabbing the volume button on the remote, she cranked up the sound as the national anthem wound down. Her eyes swept the screen, seeking number fifty-eight. Ryan glided to center ice and prepared for the face-off.

After their time at The Garden together, she saw the game—and him—in a different light. It was impossible not to. On the ice he was so serious. Focused. Driven. A born leader. She envied him that, wishing there was something in her life to be so passionate about. And off the ice? He was nothing like she would have imagined. The cocky, arrogant guy who'd flipped her bitch switch that first night? That wasn't the real Ryan.

He really was more Minnesota than New York.

An actual, honest-to-God nice guy. Something she never would have believed it she hadn't experienced it firsthand.

The puck hit the ice and the two centers jockeyed for position, trying to gain control of the puck. Ryan lost cleanly.

Cringing, Chloe reminded herself it didn't matter.

It was still too early to call the game. There were three nail-biting periods to go.

Sipping her wine, she watched for a few minutes as the two teams traded the puck back and forth, moving up and down the ice at a breakneck speed. If the first two minutes of play were any indication, it was going to be a brutal game with a whole lot of checking. And probably a fight or two.

Focusing on her work, she pulled up the list of Santa references she'd gotten from the talent agency. It was her responsibility to book the Santa for the party and she was determined to do a good job, finding a real jolly old elf, not one of those tacky looking dudes in a cheap, bright-red suit.

She peeked at the screen.

The Rangers were off to a rough start. The Pens stole the puck and were moving it down the ice. Chloe held her breath. They took a shot on goal, but it was blocked by Wright.

Shifting her attention back to the profiles, she discarded the first option immediately. Too skinny. A nice round Santa would definitely be more authentic.

The buzzer sounded, disrupting her train of thought. The Pens were celebrating when she looked up.

Damn.

Still early, she reminded herself, forcing her gaze back to the Santa profiles. She dismissed two more candidates, one for his fake beard, the other for being a smidge too fat. What good was a Santa who was too fat for kids sit on his lap?

When Chloe looked up again, Ryan was on the breakaway.

"Take the shot!" she yelled, shoving her computer aside and climbing to her knees. She leaned toward the television, holding her breath and willing the puck to find the net.

Ryan's stick came back, and he fired.

The shot was wide.

Sonofabitch!

Chloe slumped on the couch, wrapped in the overstuffed cushions.

Well, that sucked.

Ryan slashed the ice with his stick before returning to the bench.

The camera followed him, zooming in when he rubbed his calf. Was his leg bothering him? The freaking announcers seemed to think so. *Idiots.* What the hell did they know? So he wasn't on his game tonight. Maybe he was just having a bad night.

It happened, didn't it? Hopefully it wasn't anything serious.

Ryan had been working so hard.

Maybe *too* hard.

No. That was bullshit. Kelsey was wrong. And so were all of the other assmonkeys who said he was washed-up.

Ryan would fight for his career. She was sure of it.

The look in his eye when he talked about hockey? Only a fool would doubt him.

Chloe blew out a breath. Obsessing about Ryan wasn't going to get the party planned. Besides, he was a big boy. A *really* big boy. He could take care of himself.

She didn't need to mother hen him. Nor did she want to.

Pulling the computer back into her lap, she scrolled through the Santa profiles with renewed focus. Why the hell were there so many anyway? The agency must have sent her every freaking Santa they'd ever employed.

Perhaps she hadn't been clear enough. She didn't need a hundred Santa's. She just needed one really good one.

It took nearly an hour to narrow the list down, which probably had something to do with the fact that she couldn't keep her eyes off the TV. Finally satisfied with her top three choices, she settled in to watch the last few minutes of the game.

The Rangers were losing two to one, but it wasn't over yet. There were still six minutes of play. They could pull it out.

Chloe chewed on her thumbnail, eyes glued to the screen as the Blueshirts moved the puck past the red line.

Jordy passed to Ryan. Before he could make a move, one of the Pens' players slammed into him, checking him against the boards. Ryan took an elbow to the jaw, losing control of the puck.

He came off the glass swinging.

Unable to believe her eyes, Chloe watched as Ryan grabbed the jersey of the other player and delivered a right hook to his face. She sat slack jawed as the two men traded blows. The refs circled, but kept their distance. Ryan throttled the other player, pummeling him with his fists. Blood ran down his face, staining his white and black jersey. Ryan wasn't looking so hot either. His cheek was split and he was sure to end up with a massive bruise.

What. The. Fuck.

Ryan wasn't a fighter. That was Bash's job. He'd told her as much.

So what the hell did he think he was he doing?

The ref steered him toward the penalty box, but Ryan shrugged the guy off. He skated right to the players' tunnel and left the ice. Even with the heavy pads, it was clear his body was laced with tension, a live wire ready to short circuit at the smallest provocation.

Chloe cut her eyes to the clock in the upper right corner of the screen.

Her gut clenched. Less than five minutes to go. Ryan wouldn't be returning to the game.

She grabbed the remote and punched the power button. There was nothing left to see. The game was over.

Pocketing her phone, she went to bed and stretched out on top of the fluffy comforter. It didn't take a genius to figure out Ryan was probably feeling like shit. But what could she do about it? Unlike the puck bunnies she knew would be blowing up his X feed offering solace, she was four hundred miles away.

26

RYAN

FUCK IT. Ryan pushed the call button on his phone and waited. He glanced at the clock. It was late. Maybe too late. The phone rang and Chloe answered on the second ring. Even though he was glad to hear her voice, he cursed himself for caving. He should've just downed some aspirin and gone the fuck to bed. It had been a shitty night and his leg was on fire.

"Hey," she said, yawning into the phone.

Shit. He'd woken her up. "Hey," he returned, feeling like the jackass she'd accused him of being so many times. Why had he called anyway?

"Tough night," she said quietly. "How's your leg?"

"My leg is fine." He bristled, hating himself for being a defensive asshole. After all, he'd dialed her, and whether he liked it or not, it was a natural question to ask.

"Okay." She sighed, sounding frustrated. "Then how's your face?"

"I take it you saw the game?" he asked, ignoring her question.

His face was also not fine and hurt like a motherfucker, but he wasn't about to admit it. Not after he'd taken the first swing. It was just part of the game.

Of course, Bash had ripped him a new one after the final buzzer, pointing out that Ryan should've left the fighting to him.

He'd just been so damn angry. Still was. The game had been a fucking disaster. And if it wasn't bad enough that he'd played like hell, he'd gone right ahead and added poor sportsmanship to the mix, drawing a major penalty over a clean hit.

He shook his head in frustration.

So much for being a leader when his team needed him most. The only thing he'd done tonight was let them down.

Again.

"I saw the game," Chloe finally admitted. There was a quiet rustling in the background, as if she was repositioning herself, confirming his earlier assumption that she was in bed. "I had it on while I was planning for the Garden of Dreams Christmas party."

"I didn't realize your agency was handling the party," he said, surprised by the news.

Based on last year's event, it didn't seem like a big enough deal for the advertising and marketing people to be have a hand in it.

"They're not. I'm volunteering," Chloe explained matter-of-factly. "Figured I might as well put my new pseudo-celebrity status to good use and see if I can get the organization some additional press before the end of the year. Which reminds me. When are you due back in town? I miss your dick something fierce."

Grinning in spite of himself, Ryan laid back on the hotel bed, exhaustion taking over. "I've got Saturday off."

"Saturday?" she repeated, sounding so disappointed he could easily picture her bottom lip jutting out in that pouty frown she used when things weren't going her way.

"Princess, that's less than two days from now."

"Might as well be an eternity," she grumbled. "I'm horny right-*freaking*-now."

Ryan stretched his leg, flexing his ankle. A searing pain ripped through his calf, cutting off any further discussion of weekend plans. Moving the phone away from his head so Chloe wouldn't hear, he sucked in a deep breath and blew it out with controlled measure like the therapist had taught him.

Fucking A. There would probably be another visit to the doc in his future.

Just what he didn't need.

When the pain subsided, he brought the phone back to his ear. Chloe was still going strong, totally oblivious to his silence. His pride said he should be grateful she was unaware of the momentary weakness, so why was he suddenly so pissed off?

"You know what? Who says we have to wait for Saturday?" she asked, her words taking on a seductive edge. "Talk dirty to me, baby."

Ryan gritted his teeth. Any other day, he would have jumped at the challenge.

Hell, he'd have reveled in it, determined to make her come while he ordered her to finger that sweet little pussy and fulfill his every sinful suggestion. But for some reason, her request just didn't sit right with him. Anger bubbled up from his gut. Did she think sex was all he was good for? That he was just some big, dumb fucking jock that could make her come and get her extra press for her work?

If so, she didn't know the first goddamned thing about him.

Just like every other woman he'd been with.

"Come on, Ryan," she purred. "I'm naked and alone in this big old bed. And my pussy is so damn wet for you. What are you going to do about it, baby?"

Spoiling for a fight and unable to stop himself, he blurted

out the first ugly thing that came to mind. "You know there's more to life than sex, right, Chloe? And more to me? Or am I just a neat little NHL notch on your bedpost?"

She gasped as though he'd slapped her.

Then the line went dead.

A wave of molten lava rushed through his veins. He threw the damn phone across the room, not giving a shit when it cracked against the wall and clattered to the floor.

Fucking fuck.

Ryan scrubbed hand over his face and groaned, the anger ebbing from his body. He'd been a real asshole, throwing the most prickish, demeaning thing he could think of at her. To hurt her. And for what? Because he was feeling like shit. Hurting her certainly hadn't made him feel any better. If anything, he felt even smaller and less deserving than ever.

What had he expected from her anyway? Chloe wasn't his girlfriend. They weren't a thing. Hell, they barely even knew each other.

27

CHLOE

CHLOE GLARED AT HER COMPUTER, wishing the damn thing would just implode so she could go home and drown her sorrows in a bottle of wine. Or maybe a box. Yeah, a cheap box of wine would do nicely, matching her shitty mood perfectly.

Over the years, she'd suffered her fair share of indignity at the hands of the male species, but it was impossible to think of another time she'd been so completely and utterly humiliated. Because there wasn't one. She was sure of it. Never before had she put herself out there, more or less throwing herself at a guy, to have him totally shut her down—*hard*.

Talk about going down in flames.

It may have been her first attempt at phone sex, but it would also be her last, considering it had been the definition of an epic fail. No way in hell would she ever put herself in that position again. Ryan the Jerk had reared his ugly head, acting like a total asshole and treating her like some stupid, puck bunny groupie.

The memory of it made her cheeks burn.

Just because he was having a bad night, didn't mean he had to take it out on her. She'd only been trying to help, figuring sex would take his mind off the game. That's what they were about wasn't it? Why else would he have called?

She huffed out an angry breath.

A notch on her bedpost? He could take that bedpost and shove it up his—

"Morning, Chloe." Cole stood at the edge of her cubicle, leaning against the partition that separated her work space from the other Junior Associates. "How're things going with the Garden of Dreams campaign?"

"Great." She swallowed her anger, forcing a smile that was anything but authentic. "The trial run of the new spot ran at The Garden and returned over one hundred thousand dollars in donations. A few more tweaks and we'll be ready to officially roll it out." She nodded at her monitor, directing his attention to the social media analytics she was reviewing. "The online response has been strong among the test group as well."

"Good. PBA made an aggressive commitment to increase donations fifteen percent through year-end with the new campaign. We have to deliver." He gave a curt nod. "Tough game last night. How's Ryan?"

"I really wouldn't know." A hot ball of rage formed in her belly. She imagined it pulsing like a supernova, threatening to blow her apart from the inside out. Time to change the subject. "If you'll excuse me, I have a lot of work to do for Garden of Dreams today."

"My apologies," Cole said, stepping back. "I didn't mean to hold you up."

Chloe sighed, feeling like an asshole. "No, I'm sorry. I didn't mean to be rude. I'm just having a bad day. I didn't sleep very well."

"Don't give it another thought," he responded, waving off her apology and moving down the aisle.

It wasn't Cole's fault she was feeling pissy and short tempered. It was most definitely Ryan's fault. Or was it hers?

Had she gone and screwed up again, getting too invested in whatever it was she and Ryan were doing? She didn't think so. In fact, the only feelings she could muster for him were loathing, anger, and disgust.

Then again, it was impossible to see past the mountain of disdain she'd built up over the last twelve hours, so who knew? Better to not waste any more time analyzing the situation and just stick to the plan: focus on work and protect her traitorous heart at all costs.

Shoving the fight—if it could even be called that—with Ryan aside, she returned to her analytical work, promising herself she wouldn't spend her day obsessing about all the ways she was pissed off.

It worked, but damn if it wasn't exhausting.

The day had stretched interminably, and by the time five o'clock had rolled around, she'd had one foot out the door. Chloe went straight home and busted out her yoga pants and corkscrew, curling up on the couch with the remote. Flipping through the channels, she finally settled on the local news. She guzzled her wine as the blond anchor, whom she'd dubbed Susan the Smile due to her impossibly perfect teeth, rattled off the day's events.

When Ryan's face appeared in the upper right corner of the screen, she almost changed the channel. *Almost.* In the end, curiosity won out and she dropped the remote on the couch.

"New York Ranger Ryan Douglas is spreading the holiday spirit this season, promising to donate five-thousand dollars to the Garden of Dreams Foundation for each game the Rangers win through the end of the year." Susan turned to her co-anchor. "And that's not all, John, he's challenged his fellow team captains to do the same!"

The screen cut to a clip of Ryan, looking sinfully sexy in a dark polo shirt and faded jeans, speaking passionately about the work GoD was doing to serve children locally. When he flashed that panty-melting grin of his, Chloe's ovaries took notice.

"Quite a bold, and potentially expensive, move," John replied with a practiced smile. "Any word yet on whether the challenge has been accepted?"

"We haven't received an official statement from the organization or the players yet," the Smile responded. "But you can bet your jersey they're in. After all, it's a great cause. How could they say no to these faces?" she asked, flashing a picture of the kids playing hockey at The Garden with the hashtag #BlueshirtChallenge.

"Well, we certainly wish all the best to the Rangers this holiday season," John responded, wrapping up the segment.

Chloe's heart skipped a beat. The kind of press this stunt would generate couldn't be bought.

It would spread like wildfire on social media.

News and sports outlets would be talking about the challenge—and Garden of Dreams—before and after every Rangers' game for weeks. A fact Ryan surely knew, just as he knew how much Garden of Dreams meant to her. What he'd done, what he'd done *for her*, well, it was one hell of an apology. No one had ever done anything like it for her before. That didn't mean he was off the hook just yet.

They still had unfinished business.

28

RYAN

"THIS BETTER BE GOOD," Ryan muttered, dropping his beer on the kitchen counter and moving down the hall to the front door. He wasn't expecting anyone, and he was hardly in the mood for uninvited company. Throwing the lock back, he skipped the peephole and common courtesy.

"What?" he practically growled as he ripped the door open.

"Well, hey there yourself," Chloe retorted, a smug grin stretching from ear to ear, as if she knew just how miserable he'd been the last two days while she refused his calls.

For a second, Ryan just stared, processing the fact that Chloe Jacobs was standing at his front door. Uninvited. Unexpected. But totally welcome. He might've dared hope she was on the other side of the door, but he certainly hadn't expected it.

Which led to his second question. "How'd you get up here?"

Totally unfazed by his lack of manners, she shrugged. "Doorman let me up. Apparently having your face splashed all over Page Six does have its perks. Are you going to invite me in?"

"Of course. Sorry." He swung the door wide to let her pass. "I wasn't expecting anyone. You caught me a little off guard here."

"You ain't seen nothing yet," she teased, winking at him as she slipped by.

Ryan followed her to the living room, admiring the way her hips swayed as she sauntered down the hall in those fucking gold snakeskin heels that turned him inside out.

Had she worn them on purpose just to torture him?

Probably.

Chloe stopped in the center of the living room and spun on her heel, facing him. The woman was practically glowing. She was up to something. No doubt about it. Whatever it was, he sure as hell deserved it after the things he'd said to her.

He'd known his words were a dick move as soon as he'd said them, but he couldn't take them back. So he'd lain awake all night trying to think of a way to make it up to her. The challenge was the only thing he could think of to show her he was sorry. He knew how much the Garden of Dreams account meant to her, both personally and professionally. So he'd taken a chance and hoped for the best.

"It's good to see you," he said, closing the distance between them. And it was. With a winter flush in her cheeks and those wild curls, she was as beautiful as he'd ever seen her. "I wasn't sure you'd want to see me."

She raised her brow but said nothing.

"I'm sorry I was such a dick the other night," he said, pulling her body to his and loving the way she fit against him perfectly, as if she were made for him alone. He went to work on her coat, starting with the top button. "I was completely out of line. I was having a bad night and my leg was killing me, but that's no excuse for how I behaved or for how I spoke to you. You didn't deserve to be treated that way and if you never wanted to see me again, I'd understand." He searched her eyes, looking for anger, forgiveness, anything, as he worked his way through the remaining buttons. "I'm hoping you'll give me another chance. Nothing like that will ever happen again. I promise."

"I may be able to find it in my heart to forgive you," she said, slipping out of her coat and letting it fall to the floor. "But you're going to have to work for it."

Ryan's gaze slid down her bare shoulders and over the mounds of her breasts, his brain short-circuiting at the realization that the woman was not wearing any clothes. It was thirty-five fucking degrees outside and all she had on was the tiniest black lace corset and a pair of string bikini underwear. Paired with those sheer thigh highs and gold heels? It was the hottest damn thing he'd ever seen.

Fuck, yeah. He'd work for it all right.

He'd been prepared to grovel, but this was a far more interesting proposition.

Snaking an arm around his neck, she drew him in for a kiss, her tongue skating over his lips. His cock responded immediately. Needing to touch her, he deepened the kiss, running his hands over her hips and lacing them around her waist. His fingers skimmed over the barely there panties, kneading the soft flesh of her backside.

A low moan rolled from her lips and she melted against him.

Damn he'd missed this, missed her.

"So, I'm just going to let myself out. You know, before things get totally X-rated up in here. You kids have fun tonight and don't do anything I wouldn't do."

Ryan froze, realizing too late he'd forgotten all about his other visitor. Shifting his body to block Wright's view of Chloe, who'd become frozen in his arms, he gave his smart-ass teammate the finger.

They didn't need words. The message was clear: *worst timing ever, asshole.*

A few seconds later, the door to the apartment opened and closed, signaling his departure.

"You've got to be fucking kidding me. Karma, you dirty bitch!" Chloe shrieked. She dropped to the floor and grabbed her coat. She hastily stuffed her arms into the sleeves. "Please tell me that did not just happen? I am going to die of embarrassment. Seriously. Why didn't you tell me you had company?" she asked, pinning him with an anxious glare.

Ryan grabbed her hands, preventing her from buttoning the coat. "I didn't exactly know you were naked under there. And once I knew? Believe me, Wright was the last thing on my mind."

"It wasn't supposed to happen like this." She pulled her hands away and went to work on the buttons again. "They make it look so freaking easy in the movies."

"Trust me, it was a great surprise." He stroked her cheek, relishing the softness of her skin. "Don't leave."

"How can you even think about sex right now?" she asked, incredulous.

He looked her up and down. Wasn't it obvious?

She rolled her eyes and then froze. "If this ends up on Page Six—"

"First of all, Wright's not going to say a word about this —*ever*. Second of all, trust me, he's very jealous right now. You look amazing. And if you leave now, you will be solely responsible for the abuse I'll have to inflict on my body in the shower."

"I can live with that," she said, buttoning her coat and backing down the hall. She paused at the front door. "Consider it your penance."

"Princess, I'm going to consider it foreplay because this little fantasy? It's going to happen. And next time? There will be no escape."

29

——————

CHLOE

RYAN LET OUT A LOW WHISTLE. "IMPRESSIVE" seemed inadequate to describe the party Chloe and the other volunteers had put together for the Garden of Dreams families. More like mind-blowing. The banquet hall had been transformed into a Winter Wonderland, complete with Santa's workshop and... Was that a stable?

No way. It couldn't possibly be. But, yeah, there was an honest-to-God reindeer prancing around the pen, a carrot dangling from its mouth.

Reindeer in New York City? Now he'd officially seen it all.

Spotting Chloe, he made a beeline for the diminutive holiday cheer-tator who appeared to be handing out assignments to the other volunteers and guiding them to their stations. The families would be arriving soon and judging from the looks of it, the organizers were expecting a big turnout. She worked her way through the entire list without calling his name.

"What can I do to help?" he asked, stepping forward as the last of the volunteers dispersed.

Her head jerked up, and surprise washed over her face, that sexy little mouth of hers forming a perfect O.

He winked, liking the fact that he'd caught her off guard this time.

"I didn't know you were volunteering today," she said, clamping her mouth shut. Her eyes darted to the clipboard in her right hand. "Your name isn't on the list."

"Merry Christmas to you, too." He gave her a lopsided grin, which earned him an eye roll.

"Merry Christmas, Ryan. Your name isn't on the list."

"I was a last-minute addition." He leaned down, whispering conspiratorially. They were so close he could smell her perfume, and... sugar cookies? *Yum.* "Surely you aren't going to turn away a perfectly good pair of hands due to a technicality? Where's your Christmas cheer?" he teased, flicking the bell that dangled from the end of her green elf hat.

"I have cheer," she replied, planting a hand on her hip and shifting her weight. She pointed to the hat. "If this ain't holiday cheer, I don't know what is. And, no, we aren't turning away able-bodied labor, list or no list. We're shorthanded, and the families will be thrilled to see you." She chewed her bottom lip, as if deciding what to do with him. A not so innocent grin spread across her face, sending up warning flares in his brain. "Do you mind helping out with the food? Some of the trays are monstrous, and I'm sure the ladies would be thrilled to have a big strapping hockey player to help with the heavy lifting."

Sounded easy enough, and he was happy to work wherever he was needed. "I'm on it. Just point me in the right direction."

An hour later, Ryan knew exactly why he'd been assigned to help with food.

Sure, his muscles were an asset when it came to lifting the hot, steamy trays, but damn if the women weren't frisky. He'd has his ass pinched or patted no less than a half dozen times, once by a woman old enough to be his own grandma. Although it was harmless, disturbing didn't even begin to cover it.

"Having a holly-jolly good time?" Chloe asked, slipping an apron over her head.

"Why do I get the feeling you were on the naughty list this year, princess?"

"I'm sure I don't know what you mean," she replied, turning doe eyes on him.

He might've believed her, too, if only she'd been able to keep the shit-eating grin off her face.

"My ass."

Chloe burst into a fit of giggles, doubling over at the waist. "And what a fine ass it is."

Pretending to be flattered by the attention, he puffed out his chest. "That does seem to be the general consensus."

They worked side by side for the next hour, filling plates and chatting with the families who passed through the serving line.

When Chloe wasn't looking, Ryan slipped the kids extra cookies. It was tradition. He did the same thing for his nieces and nephews back home and he hadn't been caught yet.

Just one of the many advantages of having quick hands.

"What's so funny?" Chloe asked, stepping up beside him.

"Nothing. Just thinking about my family," he confessed, uncovering a fresh tray of perfectly frosted sugar cookies shaped like snowmen. "This is the first year I haven't been home for Christmas, which, as the youngest of six kids, is kind of a big deal. My parents go a little crazy around the holidays. So crazy, in fact, they've got eleven Christmas trees."

Her eyes grew wide. "Did you say eleven?"

"Yes, eleven." He glanced at his watch. "Right about now they're probably diving into my mom's famous eggnog cheesecake."

Chloe scrunched up her nose.

"What?" he asked. "You don't like eggnog."

"You do?" She shuddered. "I didn't think people actually

consumed eggnog in real life. Must be a Midwest thing. Your family sounds great though."

Ryan laughed. "It's always memorable, that's for sure. Which is why I was actually kind of dreading spending the holidays in the city, but they're shaping up better than I could have hoped." Shifting his body so Chloe wouldn't see, he slipped Isaiah two extra cookies and brought his finger to his lips, signaling it was a secret. "Being part of this event and spending the day with the kids? Totally worth it."

She nodded like she understood, and maybe she did. Her involvement with GoD had morphed from a job to a passion in a matter of weeks.

"So, what kept you in the city this year?" she asked, dumping a basket of rolls into the buffet and smiling at the young girl who reached up to grab one. "Merry Christmas, Janelle."

"Our game schedule is pretty tough this week. I couldn't risk getting jammed up in Minnesota with all of the other holiday travelers. Besides, I need the extra training." He gritted his teeth. "What about you? Where's your family today?"

Bouncing around like a pinball, she moved from the rolls to the condiments and busied herself refilling the dishes. "My parents are vacationing in the Caribbean. The holidays aren't really a big deal in my family. I'm exactly where I wanted to be today." She offered him a sympathetic smile. "I'm sorry you couldn't make it home for Christmas. That totally sucks reindeer balls."

30

CHLOE

CHLOE KNOCKED on the dressing room door for the second time, wondering what the hell was taking Santa so long. And for the second time, there was no answer.

"Third time's the charm," she grumbled, pounding on the door with the palm of her hand. "Let's go, Santa. We've got lots of good little boys and girls out here who can't wait to meet you."

Still no reply.

Deciding to take matters into her own hands, she tested the knob, hoping like hell the old guy was dressed. She had zero—make that less than zero—interest in seeing the jolly old elf in the buff. The door swung open and Chloe let herself in, closing it behind her. The last thing she needed was for one of the kids to see Santa parading around in his underpants. And why was it so damn dark?

Feeling along the wall, she searched for the light switch, flipping it with gusto when she finally found it. Fluorescent light spilled down, illuminating the couch where Santa lay sprawled out with his pants around his ankles.

"Santa?" Chloe's stomach dropped.

What was wrong with him? Was his chest moving? She couldn't be sure.

Not good.

She rushed to his side, hoping like hell the old guy was catching a nap, because she really didn't want to explain the alternative. Approaching the couch, she noticed something white peeking out of his jacket pocket. It sort of looked like a—wait, was that a prescription bottle?

Surely not. She'd done her homework. Looked at over a hundred profiles. Checked references. The agency said he was the best!

No way her Santa was a pill head.

Throwing privacy out the window, she snatched the bottle from his pocket and scanned the label. Yeah, he really was. And the dude was out cold.

She poked him in the shoulder and got an incoherent groan for her efforts.

"What the fuck, Santa?" She poked him again, harder this time. "Get your jolly ass off that couch right this minute."

He didn't budge. Eventually he managed to peel one eye open. "You're a hot little elf, aren't you?"

"You are a disgrace to Santa's everywhere," she said, pocketing the bottle.

What was she going to do? She couldn't send him out there like this, even if he could walk on his own two feet, which she was pretty sure was an impossibility given that he was barely conscious.

No Santa? The whole party would be ruined. *Ruined.*

And it would be all her fault.

The kids would be devastated.

How could she tell them Santa wasn't coming? They'd been looking forward to the event for weeks, and for some of them the foundation's gift might be the only gift of the day.

This just wouldn't do. She had to figure it out. Like, <u>right now</u>.

She glared at the wasted Santa.

"Son-of-a-bitch-no-good-pill-popping-rat-bastard-good-for-nothing-overpaid-Rent-a-Santa!" she yelled, stomping her foot in frustration.

"Whoa. Now I know you're on the naughty list." Ryan watched her with that irritating smile of his, once again bearing witness to one of her finest moments. The man was like a freaking ninja, sneaking up on her when she least expected. "A name like that? That must get you like, a whole stocking full of coal."

"This is not the time," she said, pointing a menacing finger at him.

His eyes darted to Santa and somehow that stupid grin of his managed to get even bigger. "Looks like Santa had a little too much Christmas spirit!"

"Don't you dare laugh. Don't. You. Dare," she warned, wringing her hands. How the hell was she going to fix this? She fished the prescription bottle out of her pocket and tossed it to Ryan. "So much for references. I found this in his pocket."

He read the label and pulled out his phone, typing on the screen. When he looked up, his lips were pressed into a firm line.

"Mirapex," he explained, nodding at the incoherent Santa. "Either he's got Restless Leg Syndrome or Parkinson's. Unfortunately, side effects include daytime sleep attacks."

"Narcolepsy? You've got to be freaking kidding me." Chloe groaned and scrubbed a hand over her face. "Does it say anything about hallucinations?"

Ryan quirked his brow. "How'd you know?"

"Call it a lucky guess. What am I going to..." She eyed the sleeping Santa thoughtfully. "Take off your pants."

"Excuse me?" Ryan looked at her as if she'd suddenly grown a second head.

"Take off your pants," she ordered, reaching for the buttons on Santa's coat. "You're going to be Santa while this sad sack sleeps it off."

"You're not serious?" He snorted. "No way. I don't know the first thing about being Santa. That is literally the worst idea I've ever heard."

"I seriously doubt that," she replied, fixing him with the withering glare she'd seen on her own mother's face more times than she could count. "Ryan Douglas, you will get your ass in that suit right now." She stalked across the room and grabbed his arm, wheeling him around and cracking the door. "See all those shiny little faces out there? They are waiting for Santa and we are not going to let them down. Are we?"

"No." He sighed as if the words actually pained him. "You're right. I'll do it for the kids." The corner of his mouth twitched. "But that's your Santa. You get the suit."

"Piece of cake." Chloe grabbed the pill bottle from him and dangled it in front of Santa who, fortunately, still had one eye open. Thank Frosty for small favors. "You want your pills? I want the suit. Strip."

"If you wanna see the North Pole," he said, grabbing his balls, "all you gotta do is assssk, sweet cheeks."

Drawing on years of experience tending bar, she didn't miss a beat. "Jingle your own balls, fat boy. I just want the suit."

He threw his head back and chortled. Actually freaking chortled. And was it her imagination or did his belly shake like a bowl full of jelly?

He really was the perfect Santa. Except for the whole pill thing.

That, and being a perv.

When Santa dropped his suit on the floor and kicked it

toward Chloe, she held up her end of the bargain and returned his prescription. Far be it from her to stand between a man and his medication.

She turned to Ryan. "My work here is done. Get dressed."

Grudgingly, he slipped into the suit, stuffing one of the couch pillows into his pants to create a nice round belly over his sculpted abs. "How do I look?"

"Dashing. Or is it Dasher?" she asked, tapping her chin and pretending to think about it as he patted his stomach. "I never was good at reindeer games."

Narcolepsy Santa's leg shot out, bending at the knee and kicking Ryan square in the groin.

Chloe gasped. Then she broke out in a fit of giggles as Ryan doubled over, sounding more like Bad Santa than Old Saint Nick.

"Santa just kicked me in the balls," he growled, his cheeks flushed with anger.

Or maybe that was pain.

"Right?" Chloe snorted. "Guess Santa has a case of RLS after all."

"Sorry," Santa grumbled. "New medication."

Ryan winced and straightened his back, keeping his eyes glued to the leg that had damn near rendered him sterile.

"We've got another problem." He sniffed his sleeve. "I'm no expert, but I'm pretty sure Santa shouldn't smell like a nursing home."

Chloe ground her teeth together. Then she did the first thing that came to mind.

She grabbed a can of air freshener from the table and sprayed the crap out of him. The smell of cedar filled the room, and Ryan gagged, his eyes nearly popping out of his head. "Problem solved."

Shaking his head, he pulled on the matching hat and beard.

Then, with a determined look in his eye and not a single complaint, he rejoined the party.

"Ho, ho, ho! Merry Christmas!" he shouted.

The kids came running, squealing with delight. Their laughter was infectious, and she found herself laughing right along with them. It was the worst Santa impression she'd ever seen, but in that moment, it didn't matter.

The children loved him. And that? That mattered.

Ryan settled into the big cozy chair nestled in Santa's village, and the children lined up, taking turns climbing into his lap. Santa Ryan worked out better than she could have hoped. He already knew most of the kids by name, which took them by complete surprise. They looked up at him with such awe, such wonder. And wasn't that what the season was all about?

When he caught her eye and winked, she thought her tiny little heart might've grown a size or two. It really was the sweetest damn thing she'd ever seen.

Two hours later when he cornered her under the mistletoe and demanded a kiss, she was putty in his very capable hands.

31

CHLOE

A LITTLE VOICE in the back of Chloe's head chastised her for going home with Ryan—*again*—but she shut that bitch down, refusing to give her the satisfaction. It was Christmas and she wasn't going to spend the evening alone. Besides, after spending the day watching Ryan sneak cookies to the kids and then save her ass pinch hitting for Santa? Damn the man was hot.

I'm taking a spin on the North Pole.

I need it. And I deserve it. I don't care if I end up on the naughty list.

It was a bad idea. But it didn't have to mean anything.

Woah.

She threw the e-brake on that train wreck of a thought and gave herself a mental face palm.

It *didn't* mean anything.

He was Ryan-freaking-Douglas, NHL playmaker and sex god extraordinaire. Of course, he was also an actual honest-to-God, real-life, living breathing nice guy, the kind of man she firmly believed was an endangered species. Not that it mattered. Based on what little she knew of his ex-girlfriend, she was the polar opposite of everything he wanted in a woman.

So, yeah, whatever it was they were doing, it had an expiration date.

"Close your eyes," Ryan ordered, covering her eyes and leaving her no choice but to comply.

With a hand pressed to her back, he guided her down the hall to what her semi-functional sense of direction said was the living room. A slow flush crept over her, heating her cheeks as she remembered the last time she'd visited his apartment on a whim. Whatever he had in mind, she could rest assured they'd be alone tonight. *Probably*.

"Keep them closed," he instructed, withdrawing his hand.

There was a quiet rustle from across the room. The scent of pine teased her nose. And damn if she didn't want to peek. Just one teensy, tiny little looksee. He'd never know, right? What the hell was he up to anyway?

Before she could even crack an eyelid, Ryan's hand returned to the small of her back, resting there as if it were the most natural thing in the world.

"You'd better not be peeking," he said, brushing his lips across her ear. His tongue darted out, sliding down her earlobe and teasing her in the most erotic of caresses.

"And if I am?" she asked, a grin lifting the corners of her mouth as she squeezed her eyes tighter and pushed all thoughts of expiration dates from her head. "Will you put me on the naughty list, Santa?"

"I'd rather put you on the nice list," he whispered, swatting her bottom. The sting of his open palm roused an insatiable need that only he could satisfy. "Open your eyes."

Desperate to see what he'd been up to, Chloe blinked her eyes open.

The soft glow of twinkling Christmas lights washed over her, illuminating the darkened room. Before her stood the most amazing tree in the city. It wasn't some impeccably planned designer tree. It was the real deal, the kind with mismatched, homemade ornaments dangling from the branches and no rhyme or reason to the placement, although she had no doubt each had been hung with love. It was the kind of tree she hadn't seen since her childhood—nine feet tall with a gold star on top that even Ryan would have needed a stool to put in place.

It was perfect.

"Oh my God. Ryan, I love it." She turned to him, placing a hand on the hard muscles of his chest. "When on earth did you have time to do this?"

"Last night," he admitted, scratching the back of his head and looking entirely boyish in the process. "My mom couldn't stand the thought of me spending the holidays alone with no tree, so she packed up all the ornaments from my tree back home and shipped them here."

"That's incredibly sweet." Turning to the tree, she brushed her fingers over a pair of crisscrossed hockey sticks made from popsicle sticks. It wasn't hard to imagine a much younger Ryan sitting at the kitchen table painting them. "Did you make all of these yourself?"

Ryan stood with his arms crossed over his chest as he watched her, a wicked gleam in his eye. "If I say yes, does that improve the chances of you staying the night?"

"If you want to improve those chances, take a shower." She flashed him a taunting grin. "You smell like one of those little green tree air fresheners."

A crease formed between his brows. "Just one problem." The wicked gleam in his eye shifted, spreading to the dangerous curve of his mouth as he advanced, stalking her like a lion stalks its prey. "I hate to shower alone."

Chloe lunged right, but he was too fast, scooping her up and swinging her over his shoulder.

She squealed, trying to wiggle from his grip, but it was

pointless. The man was twice her size. When those strong arms of his locked around the back of her knees, she was toast.

"What are you going to do with me?" she asked, enjoying the warmth of his hard body against hers.

Lust pooled in her belly as she contemplated her fate.

Ryan chuckled. "Princess, what you should be asking is what *won't* I do with you?"

He carried her down the hall and into the bathroom. Stopping in front of the shower, he opened the door. Although she couldn't see what he was doing, she heard him twist the knob, releasing a fast and furious spray of water that pelted the tile.

When he finally set her feet on the floor again, steam was beginning to fill the room.

Instead of removing his own clothes, he went to work on hers, wordlessly unbuttoning her blouse with painfully slow movements. Chloe shifted her weight from one foot to the other, anxious for what was to follow. The fact that he smelled like a used car was suddenly the least of her concerns. The need to mold her body to Ryan's and feel him sink deep inside her was the only thing that mattered.

Stretching up on her toes, she grabbed the back of his neck and brought his mouth to hers, fusing their lips together as desire crashed through her body, rocking it to the core. Ryan's tongue parted her lips, probing and thrusting with delicious precision. She barely recognized the sensual moan his touch elicited from her.

Moving with greater urgency, he pushed the blouse from her shoulders, running his calloused hands down her arms. When the shirt fell away and their hands met, he laced his fingers with hers, locking them together.

A shiver ran down her spine.

Ryan's mouth left hers, burning a trail of kisses down her

chin, along her neck and over her collarbone. Delicious, sensual kisses that consumed all rational thought. Chloe unbuttoned her jeans and kicked them off.

Shifting her attention to Ryan's clothes, she grabbed the bottom of his Henley and pulled it over his head, revealing the well-muscled abs that frequented her dreams on a pretty regular basis. Then she leaned down and licked those damn abs, digging her fingers into the cut muscles of his hips and thighs as she worked her way down the length of his body.

He groaned.

She eyed the shower. Figured. Her entire apartment would fit in the spa-like oasis.

It was the most divine thing she'd ever seen in her life.

How had she missed this on her last visit? Made of a neutral gray stone, it was big enough to fit the entire damn hockey team and had one, two, three...*six* shower heads.

She nearly came on the spot.

If it meant she got to take advantage of that shower, she was more than happy to indulge in whatever steamy fantasy he had planned. Leaning one shoulder into the tiled wall, he watched appreciatively as she stripped off her bra and underwear, foregoing any attempt at a striptease to get into that orgasmic shower.

"See something you like?" he asked with a smirk, crossing his arms over his chest.

"Do you?" she returned, refusing to let him bait her.

Instead, she stepped into the shower, leaving him behind. She stood in the center of the tiled oasis, letting the hot spray massage her body from every angle. Closing her eyes, she tipped her head back, letting the tension ease from her muscles.

"Oh my God," she moaned. "This is even better than I imagined."

When she opened her eyes, Ryan stood before her looking

deliciously perfect. And naked. The powerful shoulders that had carried her just minutes ago were bare, revealing the taught muscles that supported her as if she were light as air. And his abs. The well-defined eight pack spoke to countless hours in the gym.

They should've been on the cover of a romance novel. They really were that lickable.

Unable to stop herself, she continued the full body scan, taking in his thick erection before returning to his face.

"Princess, if this is the stuff your fantasies are made of," he said, nodding at the showerheads, "you need a better imagination."

He wasn't wrong. She couldn't dream this up if she tried.

Her mouth felt as if it had been stuffed with a hundred cotton balls.

Silently, she watched as Ryan filled his palm with a sea green shower gel. He rubbed his hands together, working up a good lather. When he finally reached for her, he spun her around so she couldn't see what he was up to. Standing with her back to him, waiting for him to touch her again, she was in hell.

It felt like an eternity passed before he lowered his palms to her shoulders and began massaging them, his fingers digging deep as he worked the soft tissue.

Chloe groaned. The man had good hands. There was no doubt about it.

He worked his way down her back, his hands slipping around her belly, sliding lower and lower, stroking lazy circles across her slick skin. The ache between her legs reached a fever pitch as she stretched up on her tip toes, trying to force his hands lower still. When he found her center, he teased her opening, running a single finger back and forth with agonizing precision.

She clenched her legs, desperate for him to take her. Their

bodies slick from the shower gel, he rubbed his erection against the cleft of her ass.

Turned out, the man also had inhuman self-control.

Not that she was complaining, exactly.

Not when he grabbed one of those shower heads and lowered it to the V between her legs, letting the water pressure do glorious things to her body. Bracing her hands against the wall of the shower, she rode the wave of pleasure, her body tensing for release. Ryan rotated the shower head, angling it up. She nearly lost her mind from the change in pressure.

"Oh, Ryan," she panted, twisting around to face him, her back pinned to the wall of the shower. "If you keep that up, I'm not going to need you."

"Wrong answer," he growled, replacing the showerhead.

Sliding his hands under her ass, he lifted her up.

Then his lips were on her, his kisses consuming her every thought as he teased her opening with his erection. She bit her lip, her body preparing for another reality altering orgasm. His mouth moved down the length of her neck and across her collarbone. When his lips closed over her nipple, he sucked with such ferocity that her back bowed, the tip of his penis slipping inside of her.

He groaned, freezing in place.

"Sorry. I didn't mean to do that," he said, lowering his forehead to hers. "Fuck. You feel so good."

She caressed his cheek, hardly able to believe the words about to come out of her mouth. "It's okay. I'm on the pill." She could feel her cheeks heating up. "And I'm clean. I mean, I've been checked, so, yeah, I'm good. I mean, if you are."

"Me, too," he said, clenching his jaw as his hips shifted and he slid deeper inside of her. "Regular physicals are kind of a job requirement." He studied her with eyes so serious she'd have sworn they could see right through to her soul. "Are you sure?"

Chloe weighed her response, knowing he was giving her an out, an opportunity to change her mind. But she wouldn't take it. She trusted him. "I'm sure."

The mood in the shower shifted.

Chloe ignored the niggling voice in the back of her head that said this was a stupid move, the one that said this felt like a hell of a lot more than two adults giving one another pleasure. Ryan must've felt it, too. His kisses became deeper, harder, as he wound his fingers through her hair, thrusting deep and hard.

Gripping his shoulders, Chloe held him tight as he rocked his hips against hers, driving them both toward the explosive finale. And she knew it would be explosive. Making lo—having sex with nothing separating their bodies meant a new level of trust. For the first time, they were truly joined. Everything felt more intense, like it was their first time again.

Ryan's grip on her hips tightened, and she knew he was close.

They were going to come together. What could be more perfect than that?

The tension in her belly coiled tight, exploding from her center and sending a torrent of pleasure crashing through her body. Ryan stiffened as he gave a final thrust, driving deep, their bodies molded together. He wrapped his arms around her, holding her tight as his body sagged against hers, the tiled wall providing support for both of them.

Afterward, as Ryan washed her body again, his fingers gently working a soapy lather over her limbs, she wondered if they'd gone too far. Crossed a line, perhaps? Did it matter? Even if they had, she couldn't—*wouldn't*—bring herself to regret it.

32

RYAN

RYAN FLIPPED through the channels on the television, looking for something—*anything*—to take his mind off the thoughts that had been circling his brain all day. With Chloe curled up next to him wearing nothing but a sheet, it was impossible to ignore the obvious. Somewhere between all the bickering and the scorching hot sex, they'd become... something more.

Or did he just want something more?

Either way, it scared the hell out of him.

After everything he'd gone through with Kelsey, the idea of taking that risk again wasn't exactly appealing. But Chloe wasn't Kelsey. She was different, something she'd shown him in so many small ways over the last couple of weeks. What they could have—if she'd give him the chance—had to be worth the risk.

For both of them.

Catching the theme song for *Gremlins*, he stopped on Spike TV. Perfect. Nothing like little green monsters on Christmas to occupy the mind, right?

Chloe propped herself on one elbow, her nose scrunched up. "Of all the Christmas movies on TV, this is the one you're going to watch?"

"No," he said, pulling her close and covering her body with the sheet. "This is the one *we* are going to watch. What do you have against *Gremlins* anyway?"

He could practically see her eyes rolling when she responded. "Aside from the fact that they're murderous little beasts? The whole thing is depraved. I mean, that one chick's dad gets stuck in the chimney and dies on Christmas Eve. I swear I was terrified growing up that Santa was going to get stuck in my chimney."

"You had a chimney in the city?" he asked, knowing the odds were nil.

"Not the point," she replied with a sniff.

"Let me make sure I've got this right. No *Star Wars*. No *Star Trek*. Now no *Gremlins*?" He groaned. "We really need to work on your cinematic education. Starting right now. *Gremlins* is the best anti-Christmas holiday movie ever. It's a classic. The animatronics in this film were cutting edge back in the eighties. If they remade it today, it would be all CGI and it would completely bastardize the whole thing."

"On second thought." She snickered, snaking her arms across his belly and grabbing the remote. "Less geek talk, more Gremlins. I do love me some Gizmo."

"What's not to love?" he agreed. Reaching under the nightstand, he pulled out the box he'd wrapped earlier in the day. The woman had crap taste in movies, but it didn't change anything. It was now or never. He laid the box on her lap, hoping like hell she would understand the significance of the gesture. "Merry Christmas, Chloe."

"What's this?" Holding the sheet to her breasts, she sat up again. "You got me a present?" She licked her lips and tucked her hair behind her ear, revealing the tips of her ears had turned bright red. "I didn't get you anything."

The look of dejection on her face was like a punch to the gut.

His hand shot out instinctively, lifting her chin and forcing her to meet his eyes. "Yes, you did, Chloe. Maybe it didn't come wrapped up in a box with a shiny bow on top, but you gave me something better, something so genuine and unexpected. Something I will never forget."

She studied him with curious eyes, chewing on her bottom lip.

"You believed in me when I needed it most, when you didn't have any reason to, and when a hell of a lot of other people didn't. Your support, the support you gave so freely, meant more than you can possibly know."

"I don't know what to say."

"Don't say anything," he said, rubbing his thumb across her cheek. Leaning into his touch, she closed her eyes and slid her hand over the top of his. "Why don't you open the box?"

She nodded and pulled the bow loose, taking her sweet time opening the gift that had his heart in his throat, beating wildly. Hell, if she didn't pick up the pace, he might choke on it.

Finally, she tore the paper from the box and shook it open.

When she folded the tissue paper back to reveal the contents, her eyes grew wide.

"Is this your jersey?" she asked, pulling it from the box and spreading it over her lap. Her fingers traced the letters of his name almost reverently.

"It's from my first season with the Rangers," he explained, suddenly at a loss for words despite practicing them in his head a hundred times as he'd wrapped the gift. "I want you to have it."

"Why?"

Talk about a loaded question. Stalling, he raked his hands through his hair as he grasped for the right words. While Chloe preferred the direct approach, he was pretty sure "I want to be more than fuck buddies" was a little too insensitive for what he had in mind. "You're my girl and I want the entire world to know it. I want *you* to know it. What we have? It's good, but it can be so much better."

An eternity passed while he waited for her to say something. *Anything.*

His gut churned with unease as he wondered if he'd fucked everything up.

"I'm not sure what to say," she finally admitted, wrinkling her brow. Not exactly the reaction he was hoping for. "Won't a relationship ruin everything? Seriously. As soon as we get invested, it will all go to hell. Trust me, I'm the expert on breakups, remember? Happens every time. Besides, things are going so well. Why screw it up?"

Ryan sucked in a deep breath, knowing this wasn't something he could push, or pull, or challenge her into. If they were going to do it, they both had to be all in.

"We've both been burned in the past, but this is a chance for a fresh start. Just think about it. This thing between you and I? It's real, no matter how hard we try to deny it. Why don't we just take it slow and see where life takes us?"

Chloe smiled that thousand-watt smile of hers and slipped the jersey over her head. It was easily five times too big, but hanging off her shoulder? It was the sexiest thing in the world.

Drawing her close, he gave her a feather light kiss, their lips barely brushing. "For the record, I'm taking that as a yes."

33

RYAN

Ryan tugged at his bowtie, wishing he could take the damn thing off. He liked a good party as much as the next guy, but he would prefer to ring in the New Year without the monkey suit. The team was riding high from their win against the Panthers and the annual event was in full swing, courtesy of the team's owner. The alcohol was flowing and music pulsed through the room, threatening to blow his eardrums as the band rocked out on stage.

Next to him, Chloe was practically twitching to hit the dance floor, a giant grin plastered on her beautiful face as she swayed to the music. It was strange to think that six weeks ago she hadn't even been part of his life and now they were welcoming the New Year together. Even stranger was his willingness to join her on the dance floor, just to make her happy.

And he knew it would make her happy.

"Should've ditched the bowtie in the car," Chloe teased, straightening his tie. Leaning in close, she pressed against him, stretching up to whisper in his ear. Her breath was hot on his cheek. "I'll tell you what, if you can make it to midnight, I'll let you tie me up with that thing later tonight."

Ryan groaned, his cock responding immediately to the suggestion.

Wasn't it enough that she was wearing that sexy fucking gold dress from the first night they met? Now she had to go and throw a little bondage in the mix, as if his imagination weren't already offside?

"Challenge accepted."

"Hey, man." Jordy clapped him on the back, fashionably late and wearing a silver vest that would've looked tacky on anyone else. Somehow he managed to pull it off without looking like a complete douche. He winked at Chloe. "I've got a bottle of Patron with your name on it."

Throwing her head back, she laughed and patted his arm. "I appreciate the offer, but I'm keeping it low key tonight. Besides, I got everything I need from you, Skarkowski. Unless you were holding out on me?"

She quirked her brow, apparently reevaluating his value to her charity work.

Jordy just shrugged, looking too damn smug for his own good.

"I'm going to grab another beer. You want anything?" Ryan asked. Although Chloe shook her head in response, her eyes remained focused on Jordy. He leaned down and kissed her forehead. "Please do not accept any of his ridiculous challenges while I am gone."

"I make no promises."

Changing tactics, he turned to his teammate. "You get my girl drunk tonight and I will kick your ass."

"Your girl, huh?" Jordy tilted his head, a devious grin spreading across his face as he slung an arm around Chloe's shoulders. "Sounds like Chloe and I have some catching up to do."

Ryan rolled his shoulders.

Bringing Chloe to the team's New Year's Eve party would start a new flurry of speculation about their relationship. Not that it bothered him. He was used to being in the spotlight and had stopped giving a damn what people thought years ago. When he'd said he wanted the world to know she was his girl, he'd meant it.

Problem was, Chloe might not feel the same way.

She'd made it perfectly clear she didn't like seeing her face, or her personal life, splashed all over the papers. But that was a problem for another day. Tonight he just wanted to enjoy the party and the company of his gorgeous date. They'd have plenty of time to figure out the rest later.

"Make sure you're back before midnight." Chloe's fingers brushed his hand, sending a shiver down his spine. "With the bowtie."

It was official. The woman was trying to kill him.

Edging through the crowd, he made his way to the bar. The line was twenty deep.

He checked his watch. Plenty of time to hit the head and grab a beer before midnight.

Changing course, he slipped out of the ballroom and into the main hall. Thankfully, the heavy doors trapped most of the earsplitting music inside with the three hundred soon-to-be-deaf guests. He looked up and down the hall for the telltale restroom sign. Although he was grateful for a reprieve from the noise, he didn't want to leave Chloe alone too long. Jordy would keep her company, but there was a very real possibility one or both of them would be moving from happily buzzed to totally lit if he didn't get his ass back in there soon.

When he'd finished in the restroom and straightened the offensive bowtie for the eight thousandth time, Ryan set out for the ballroom.

He didn't get far.

"Hey, Ry." Kelsey stepped out of the shadows, blocking his path.

She wore a black dress that looked as if it had been painted on, and her hair was swept up, highlighting the perfect bone structure most people assumed came at the hand of a really good surgeon. Only Kelsey was all natural—on the outside. Inside?

That was still up for debate.

"Kelsey." He silently cursed himself for the cold, clipped tone, which had everything to do with her standing in his way, but which she was sure to interpret as lingering anger over their nuclear breakup. "To what do I owe the honor?" he asked, trying to keep he edge from his voice.

"I've been looking everywhere for you." She flashed him a coy smile and inched closer. It was the same trick she'd used to get her way a hundred times when they'd been dating. He stepped back, maintaining his distance. "We need to talk."

Ryan studied he woman who'd broken his heart and stripped him of his confidence and he felt...nothing. Gone was the burning anger, the humiliation, the resentment. All he felt was pity.

And relief.

If he hadn't been hurt, if she hadn't left, well, he might not have found himself. Or Chloe.

His chest tightened at the thought. In the short time he'd known her, she'd become as integral as his next breath. The idea that his life could have gone on as it was before—*without her in it*—was unfathomable.

"I'm not in the mood to talk, Kelsey." Ryan crossed his arms over his chest. "Besides, you said more than enough the last time we spoke."

"You don't have to talk, just listen," she said, closing the gap between them. Only inches remained between their bodies. "I made a mistake Ryan. You and I? We belong together. Let's try again. New year, new start."

"You're drunk," he charged, unable to believe his ears or his eyes. Did she really think he would just roll over and thank his lucky stars for a second chance? That he'd forget everything that had happened in the last five months? "Don't do this, Kels. Don't do this to Bash. He loves you."

"I don't want to talk about Bash. I don't love Bash," she said, dragging a perfectly manicured nail down his chest. His heart hammered in response. This little talk was going from bad to worse. "I want to talk about us. I love you."

He grabbed her wrist to prevent any further exploration of his body. Those days were long gone and he had no interest in going back. *Ever.*

"It's too late. I've moved on. I'm happy with Chloe, a woman who actually gives a shit about me and not my bank account."

Kelsey laughed, a bitter, derisive sound sliding from her lips like poison. "You've had your fun. Now it's time to think about your future. Dating a professional hockey player? Come on, Ry. You know it takes a strong woman. Do you really think Chloe is up to the challenge? With the long seasons? The road games? Puck bunnies? The paparazzi?"

His gut twisted, hating the faint truth of her words.

Hadn't he wondered the same thing himself? Would his lifestyle bring Chloe a world of heartache? *No.* He wouldn't let that happen. And why was he even having this discussion? It was time to get his ass back to the party and Chloe's side.

That was the only place he wanted to be tonight.

"Happy New Year, Kelsey. Have a good night."

"Oh, I will." She smiled and stepped around him, tripping unceremoniously on her dress. Or maybe she'd just had too damn much to drink.

Whatever the cause, instinct kicked in and Ryan reached for

her, catching her around the waist and preventing any serious damage. Her hands found his chest again, braced against his body as she sought purchase. She beamed up at him as though he were the sun to her moon, just like the old days. And then she brought her mouth to his, as if she meant to kiss him.

"What are you doing?" he yelled, extricating himself from her grasp and pushing her away an instant before those familiar lips brushed his.

Kelsey straightened her back, looking up at him with sad eyes. Her shoulders rose and fell as if the weight of the world rested upon them. "It was worth a shot."

"I told you, I'm happy with Chloe." He dragged a hand through his hair, trying to sort out his thoughts.

Why the hell had Kelsey tried to kiss him? Hadn't he been clear? The only woman he wanted to kiss was Chloe.

Chloe.

His stomach dropped. She'd be wrecked if she thought he were sneaking around with Kelsey. And it would wreck him to hurt her like that. Would she believe him if he told her the truth? He wasn't sure. Their relationship was too new, too fragile. She'd barely agreed to give him a chance.

Something like this? It would send her running. He knew it in his gut.

She'd write him off as another douchebag athlete who broke her heart. He couldn't let that happen, not when things were going so well between them. A glance up and down the hall confirmed he and Kelsey were alone, something he'd ensure never happened again.

"Stay the hell away from me, Kelsey. Just stay away."

34

CHLOE

Chloe scanned the room, searching for Ryan. It was nearly midnight and she was determined to ring in the New Year right, kissing those sinful lips of his, no matter how surreal the whole thing felt. And to think just weeks ago she'd sworn off men, vowing she'd never date another athlete.

Life was funny like that sometimes, giving you just what you needed when you least expected it. She still had moments of doubt, those niggling little voices that said Ryan would never truly be hers, or that he would tire of her and trade her in for a blond model, but for now, she was giving him—*them*—the benefit of the doubt.

The way he made her feel? It was worth the risk. It had to be.

Weaving her way through the crowded room, she gave silent thanks for the five-inch stilettos that pinched her toes. Even with the added height, most of the guests seemed to tower over her.

Fortunately, Ryan kind of stood out in a crowd.

Seeing him approach from the other side of the dance floor, still wearing the bowtie, she grabbed two flutes of champagne from a passing waiter. This would be the best New Year's Eve ever.

"Took you long enough," she teased, when he reached her side empty handed. "What? Did they run out of beer? No worries. I grabbed champagne for the toast."

"Thanks." Ryan accepted the glass, looking distracted.

It was impossible to miss the tension that laced his shoulders, especially when he lifted the flute to his mouth and drained it, not bothering to wait for midnight.

Chloe raised her brow, but said nothing. Instead, she reached up and straightened his tie again. The damn thing seemed to have a mind of its own.

She grinned, thinking about her earlier promise to Ryan. There was no doubt he'd hold her to her word. Her belly fluttered at the thought of the soft black material wrapped around her wrists.

The MC took the stage and all eyes turned to the front of the room.

With a few pretty words and a flick of the wrist, Times Square lit up the stage, projected on a larger-than-life screen. *Eleven fifty-nine.* Chloe's breath hitched in her throat when Ryan slipped an arm around her waist and pulled her flush to his side. Heat radiated from his body, raising her own body temperature instantly. Or maybe that was hormones? That was probably it.

A dangerous tingle spiraled through her body and she found herself admiring his profile instead of watching the countdown.

Ten.

Nine.

Ryan's body turned, his gaze locked on hers.

Eight.

Seven.

The way he was looking at her... Oh, God. It was like she was the only woman on the planet, stripped bare for him alone.

Six.

Five.

Chloe's body was on fire.

Four.

Three.

She couldn't breathe.

Two.

One.

The room exploded. *Auld Lang Syne* drifted from the stage. Fireworks burst from the Times Square feed. Confetti rained down from above. It was sensory overload, but all the sights and sounds paled in comparison to what she felt when Ryan touched her.

His touch was gentle as he brought his hand to her cheek and lifted her chin to him, his eyes burning right through her as his lips descended.

It was the kind of kiss she'd always longed for. Tender. Sensual. *Possessive.*

Some rational part of her brain reminded her they weren't alone, and that this kiss went beyond a chaste PDA, but she didn't care. Couldn't care. Not when Ryan was holding onto her like she was his last breath. It was the most amazing feeling in the world. In all her life she'd never experienced anything like it.

Was it possible love had actually found her when she'd finally stopped looking?

35

CHLOE

CHLOE SAT on the edge of her seat, a swarm of butterflies doing a number on her belly. She wiped her palms on her skirt, anxious for the Garden of Dreams executives to finish their introductions and wrap up the New Year's pleasantries with the other PBA team members. She didn't need perfunctory good will from the board members, she needed GoD's fourth quarter results.

After all, it was January second. Happy New Year was so yesterday.

Fortunately, Cole was much better at politicking. He appeared perfectly at ease chatting about resolutions that wouldn't last the week while it took a herculean effort for her to smile politely and laugh at all the right moments. Especially when all she really wanted was to go Jerry Maguire on their asses and yell 'show me the money'.

There were several A-list actors on the board. Who knew— maybe they'd appreciate the dramatics.

When the GoD board finally passed around the presentation deck, Chloe left her copy untouched on the table in front of her. Unprofessional or not, there was no way she'd be able to stop herself from flipping ahead if she opened it. She was dying to know if the campaign—and all of her extra fundraising efforts—had delivered. She'd worked so damn hard on the campaign.

Now it was time to find out if all that hard work had paid off.

Under the table, her phone buzzed in her bag.

She ignored it, doing her best to focus on the speaker who was droning on and on about the financial challenges GoD had faced earlier in the year. No surprises there. It was the exact reason they'd hired PBA. Everyone in the room knew it.

The damn phone buzzed again. Even on silent, the vibration was a distraction in the quiet boardroom. A few heads turned her way.

So much for being discreet.

Shifting in the soft leather chair, she pushed the bag further under the table, knowing it wouldn't actually help. When it buzzed again not thirty seconds later, she reached under the table and pulled the bag into her lap.

"I'm terribly sorry for the interruption," she said, fishing for the phone and shutting it off without looking at the screen. "Please continue."

Cole shot her a questioning glance. She shrugged.

Whoever it was could wait. If it were a true emergency, they'd call the office and Cole's admin would pull her out of the meeting. Gabby was nowhere to be seen, so it was probably nothing.

The speaker, whose name she couldn't pronounce if her life depended on it, cleared his throat and continued. "The push Garden of Dreams received from the PBA campaign tipped the scales in the fourth quarter. Donations increased by nineteen percent." Pausing, he pushed his glasses up the slope of his nose. "In fact, media coverage for the Christmas party was so strong, Garden of Dreams received record donations the week of the holiday."

"That's fantastic news," Cole said, gesturing to Chloe. All eyes swung in her direction. Heat flooded her cheeks. No doubt she was grinning like a fool, but it didn't matter. Record donations? She kind of wanted to do a happy dance right on the table. The phrase "high on life" suddenly took on a whole new meaning. The butterflies that had been fluttering around in her belly had taken flight, fanning out through her body with a burst of adrenaline. "I told you my team would deliver."

"We are incredibly pleased with the results, given the compressed timeline. I should also warn you that we'll be looking for even bigger gains next year."

Cole laughed good-naturedly and the rest of the team followed his lead. The time for pressure would come later. Today was about celebrating a job well done.

She couldn't wait to tell Ryan.

After all, he'd played a key role in raising awareness and donations with his Blueshirt Challenge.

When the meeting wrapped up and there were no more attaboys to be handed out, Chloe headed back to her desk, walking on air. Double-digit growth in the fourth quarter? That was huge. No one could say PBA hadn't delivered, but mostly she was excited about what it would mean for the foundation. More money meant more resources for more children. Her heart swelled with pride, knowing her work would help change thousands of lives throughout the tri-state area.

Back at her desk, she dug her phone out of her bag and pushed the power button.

What was so important it had been blowing up during the meeting?

The screen flashed to life and her jaw nearly hit the desk. Eighteen text messages, four missed calls, and a pile of notifications on all of her social media accounts? She glanced at the clock. It had only been, what? Thirty minutes?

The adrenaline that had her soaring just moments ago soured in her veins.

Sucking in a deep breath, she collapsed in her chair, hugging the phone to her chest. It was bad news, no doubt about it. But how bad?

Only one way to find out.

Unlocking the phone, she scrolled to Olivia's texts first. There were three of them. All sent back-to-back. Definitely not good.

Call me.

Have you seen Page Six?

Are you okay? CALL ME!

Heart racing and hands shaking, she gripped the edge of the desk, using it for support as she rose to her feet. She needed *The Post*. Like, now.

There would be a copy in reception, assuming no one had taken off with it already.

Walking down the aisle, she felt dozens of eyes following her every move. The whispers were even less subtle. Squaring her shoulders, she lifted her chin, cursing the stupid cubicle farm.

When she stepped into the reception area, the girl behind the desk said nothing and handed her a copy of the paper, a look of pity in her eyes. Tucking the paper under her arm, she returned to her cube, refusing to acknowledge the whispers that trailed her every step.

Chloe spread the paper on her desk.

How bad could it really be? She was probably overreacting. Getting herself worked up over nothing. Her heart slammed against her rib cage, refusing to indulge her with even a moment of wishful thinking.

Relaxing her breathing, she flipped to Page Six.

And right there in black and white were two pictures of Ryan.

One of him kissing her at midnight on New Year's Eve. They looked so happy. So in love. So perfect. She touched his face, dragging her fingers to the next picture, the one that shredded her heart and punched a hole in her soul. A hole she was sure could never be mended. Ryan holding Kelsey on New Year's Eve. Her hands were fisted in his jacket, his bowtie askew, their mouths just a breath apart, as if they were about to kiss.

Chloe's stomach dropped and anger blazed through her as she read the headline: Douglas headed to the penalty box?

Forcing herself to read the article, she skimmed the highlights, each one like a knife planted deep between her shoulder blades.

"Looks like New York Ranger Ryan Douglas is playing more than hockey..." Tears welled up behind her eyes. She would not cry. Not here. "Chloe Jacobs is yesterday's news..." She wanted to throw up. Just not in the trashcan. "Sources close to Kelsey Cruise, Douglas's longtime girlfriend, say she and Douglas are committed to working through their differences..."

This could not be happening.

Humiliation stung her cheeks. She needed to get out of there. *Fast.*

Arms wrapped around herself, Chloe hightailed it to the elevator.

When she reached the ground floor and stepped out onto Madison Avenue, it was clear she wouldn't be suffering the latest indignity of her love life in private. The paps descended like vultures, snapping pictures and peppering her with invasive and provocative questions.

"Chloe, did you and Ryan have an open relationship?"

"Are you going to fight for your man?"

"Did you know he was reconciling with Kelsey Cruise?"

A tall, greasy looking man stepped in front of her, thrusting a microphone in her face. "Now that Ryan's done slumming, how do you feel about being used?"

Anger coursed through her veins. She closed her fist, tensing to strike.

No one would blame her if she throttled the guy. But that was the point, wasn't it? To get her acting out on video. To have her make headlines of her own. To fuel the fire. It was a desperate attempt to get a sound bite.

Her brain told her as much, but that didn't make it any less painful.

Biting her tongue, she stuffed her fists in her pockets and prayed she could hold the tears back long enough to throw herself into a cab.

Five minutes later, tucked in the back of a Yellow Cab and crawling across town at a snail's pace, she dialed Liv. Thankfully, she answered on the first ring.

"Where are you?" she demanded, her words filled with concern. "Are you okay?"

"Cab. I don't know." Chloe slouched against the seat, the morning's rollercoaster of events taking its toll on her. She sniffed, wiping the back of her hand across her eyes, not giving a damn whether her waterproof mascara held up. "I can't believe this is happening."

"Maybe it's not what it looks like?" Liv suggested, sounding doubtful.

Chloe appreciated her attempt at positivity, but this was the real world and not some stupid rom-com. She wasn't his—or anyone else's—exception. It was that kind of thinking that got her into this mess in the first place.

"Come on, Liv. It's exactly what it looks like. Pictures don't lie." A bitter laugh tumbled from her lips. "I'm such a fool. I knew this would happen. I *knew* it. And like an idiot, I just kept falling, letting myself get swept up in his stupid life. In his lies.

What was I thinking? Why would he ever stay with me when he can have any woman he wants?"

"Maybe you should talk to him, hear his side of things," Olivia suggested. "But I'm telling you right now, if he did this, then he doesn't deserve you. Hell, he doesn't deserve to breathe the same air you do."

"Says the best friend on cue." Chloe closed her eyes. Was this all her life would be? Good enough for a fling, but never a ring?

"I'm coming over. I'll meet you at your place."

"No," Chloe said, pinching the bridge of her nose. "I just want to be alone. Please, just leave me alone."

36

RYAN

RYAN PULLED his practice jersey over his head, anxious to hit the ice. The doc had given him a wicked stretch and he was feeling pretty damn good. Maybe he really was turning the corner in his recovery. With the holidays behind them and more than forty games remaining in the regular season, the team's focus was on securing a playoff berth.

Hell, he could hardly believe he'd be part of it given the way he'd started the season.

He glanced up as the locker room door opened.

Bash. And he did not look happy.

Ryan had only seen that look once before, during their college days when Bash's parents had announced their divorce. "Hey, man. Everything okay?"

Bash narrowed his gaze at Ryan and charged.

For a big guy, he moved fast, covering the space between them in two quick strides. Pinned between the lockers and the bench, Ryan was trapped. A feral growl roared in his ears as Bash's meaty hands grabbed the front of his jersey and slammed him against the lockers. His back smashed against the metal, his head bouncing off the smooth surface.

"What the fuck is your problem?" he yelled, bringing his arms up between Bash's to try and drive the bigger man's arms apart.

No dice. Bash had a death grip on the damn jersey.

"Why'd you do it?" Bash yelled, his dark eyes brimming with anger. That same anger seemed to permeate his body, each of his limbs fraught with tension. "Why the fuck did you do it, man?"

"I don't know what you're talking about." Lowering his voice in an attempt to deescalate the situation, he dropped his arms, hoping like hell his teammate wouldn't take a shot at him.

He'd made it this far with all his teeth intact, and he preferred to keep it that way.

"Kelsey," Bash said, slamming Ryan's body against the lockers as if to emphasize his point.

Ryan sighed. Of course. What the fuck had she done now?

"Like I said, I have no idea what you're talking about. You're going to have to clue me in."

"I love her." Bash's voice dropped to a whisper as the fight left his body. "I fucking love her."

Taking advantage of his relaxed posture, Jordy and Bischoff jumped in, grabbing Bash's arms and pulling him free of Ryan. Watching Bash with a wary eye, Ryan rotated his shoulder and adjusted his jersey. Apparently the only thing hurt was his pride.

Bash dropped to the bench, looking defeated.

Finally, he reached into his back pocket and pulled out a rolled-up newspaper. He threw it at Ryan, a disgusted look carved on his face.

The locker room was deathly quiet, the other players watching them, waiting to see how the fight would play out. Ryan cut his eyes at Jordy, who was poised to jump back in if needed.

Confident he wouldn't get sucker punched, he unrolled the paper.

Page-fucking-Six. It was starting to be a real pain in his ass.

It was also starting to feel like someone over there had a hard-on for the Rangers. They couldn't catch a break.

His gut clenched when he saw his own face staring back at him.

Two pictures. Two women. One night.

He didn't need to read the article to know what it said. Or what Bash thought. What Chloe would think.

Chloe.

A new feeling blossomed in his gut. *Fear.*

"*FUCK*," he roared, balling the paper up and throwing it at the wall. "Fuck, fuck, fuck."

Molten lava flowed through his veins, searing a path from his gut to his head, burning up all rational thought. Overwhelmed by the intensity of his feelings, and fighting for control, his body vibrated with energy.

Not good.

His head was going to fucking explode if he didn't find a physical outlet for his rage. *Fast.*

He drew back his fist and let it fly, punching his locker and denting the door.

Pain shot up his arm. It paled in comparison to the ache in his chest.

Maybe Chloe hadn't seen the article yet. Maybe he could do damage control.

If he got to her first, she'd understand. He'd make her understand.

Grabbing his bag, he dug out his phone.

It was his own fault, he realized, as he punched in the access code. He should've just told her about Kelsey's stupid behavior on New Year's Eve. He should've been honest with Chloe and Bash, but he hadn't wanted to hurt anyone.

And look how well that had turned out.

Odds were they both hated his guts right now.

His heart sank as he scanned his phone. The story was all over the web. There was no way Chloe hadn't seen it yet.

After all, she was a social media guru. She lived and breathed this stuff.

Disgusted, he threw the phone back in the bag and turned to Bash.

"It's bullshit," he said, looking his friend in the eye. "There is nothing going on between me and Kelsey. She had too much to drink New Year's Eve and made a pass at me. I told her to take a walk. She tripped, I caught her. End of story."

"Apparently not." Bash shook his head and scrubbed his hands over his face. "You really expect me to believe that?"

Ryan shrugged. It was the truth, and it was all he had to offer. Pointing out that Kelsey had set him up with zero consideration for Bash's feelings wasn't going to help. She'd already screwed him over ten ways to Sunday. No need to rub salt in the wound. Hell, she'd screwed them all over. "I'm sorry you had to find out like this, but I promise you there is nothing going on between us. And there never will be. I love Chloe."

Shit.

He loved Chloe.

And she would probably never speak to him again.

37

RYAN

RYAN CLIMBED the stairs to Chloe's apartment, willing her to be home. It was the first time he'd been back in the city since that damn article had run on Page Six. The team had gone straight from the Tarrytown practice facility on a road series, and she'd been ignoring his calls and texts for days.

He was worried about her. Really worried.

She hadn't responded to a single message. Not one.

Not to ask if it was true. Not to tell him to stay away. Not even to call him a son-of-a-bitching-no-good-lying-rat-bastard-piece-of-shit-cheater or whatever colorful name she could come up with.

The silence was worse. More painful, somehow. As if it carried an echo of finality.

Final his ass. He wouldn't accept it. Couldn't. He'd talk to her —make her see reason. The alternative had his gut twisted in anxious knots.

Stopping in front of her door, he wiped his palms on his jeans and drew a deep breath. He needed to center himself, just as he did before a game. One way or another, she was going to talk to him. Even if it meant he had to sit in front of her damn door all night.

He knocked.

No answer.

He knocked again.

This time he heard footsteps beyond the door. She was definitely home. Whether or not she would willingly answer was an entirely different question. "Chloe, please open the door. I know you're home."

Nothing.

Time for the bold approach. "I've got all night and I'm not leaving until you talk to me."

"Go away." Her reply was muffled, but he was willing to bet she was just on the other side of the door.

"Not happening." Mere inches separated them, but it felt like miles. He needed her to see her. Needed to see her beautiful face, to look into her eyes. Then maybe she'd know the truth of his words. "Like I said, I've got all night. I hope your neighbors don't mind." He paused, letting her contemplate the prospect of him camping in her hallway. "Fair warning, I've been known to sing to pass the time. Loudly."

There was a *thunk* on the other side of the door, as though she'd banged her head against it in resignation. He wasn't exactly looking for resignation, but if it got her to open up, he'd take it.

Thwack!

Ryan's pulse quickened at the sound of the lock being disengaged. When she finally opened the door, his heart stopped. His girl—the gorgeous, spunky, fearless woman he'd come to cherish—was nowhere to be seen. In her place stood a woman who looked lifeless, defeated, and utterly dejected. She'd been crying. Even without the tear tracks, he'd have seen it in her puffy, red-rimmed eyes.

He'd done that to her. To the woman he loved. And it broke his heart.

When he reached for her, she jerked away, her body stiffening. The wide-necked sweatshirt she wore slid off her shoulder, revealing the smooth, silky skin he'd kissed so many times before.

"Don't. Touch. Me."

Withdrawing the offending hand, he shoved his fists in the pockets of his jeans. The eyes he'd expected to flash with anger were flat, closed off to emotion. Closed to him. He couldn't read her. She'd lost more than her usual sparkle. Gone were the larger-than-life emotions she typically wore on her sleeve. He'd been prepared for pissed off, screaming, even for a kick in the nuts if she felt so inclined. But he hadn't been prepared for this. Not in the least.

Unsure of what to say, he decided to start with the obvious. "We need to talk."

She just stared at him with that goddamned blank look, arms crossed over her chest.

Fuck. Not even an eye roll? He was so screwed.

"What you saw on Page Six, it wasn't—" He growled in frustration, feeling like a damn heathen as he stood before her, wanting nothing more than to toss her pert little behind over his shoulder and lock her in the apartment. At least until he could make her see it his way. "It wasn't what it looked like."

The brittle laugh that spilled from her lips set his teeth on edge. "Really? All this time to think and that's the best you could come up with? How original."

"It's the truth," he said, removing his hat and tucking it in his back pocket. He raked a hand through his hair. "And if you'd answered my calls, I'd have told you days ago. Maybe saved us both a little heartache."

"Oh, no you don't," she said, jabbing him in the chest with

her pointer finger. Suddenly those flat eyes were alive, a raging inferno burning bright. "You do not get to pretend like this is hurting you, too, like you actually give a damn. You did this." She poked him in the chest again. "And you know what the worst part is? I let you. I was actually stupid enough to believe it when you said you wanted me to be your girl. That you wanted the world to know." She shook her head, a look of disgust contorting her face. "Why'd you do it, Ryan? Why ask me to be your girl if you were getting back together with Kelsey?"

"I am not getting back together with Kelsey. Ever."

Did she really believe that? After everything he'd told her?

"Oh, you were just sucking her brains out through her mouth then? Is that supposed to make me feel better?" She snorted. "You know, the least you could have done was told me yourself, instead of making me into some pathetic fucking club joke. Do you have any idea what they're saying about me online? What kinds of messages I'm getting? It's a total shit show. But I guess you don't give a damn, right? You had your fun, and now you get to move on with your perfect goddamned Barbie doll and your perfect goddamned life."

"I did not kiss Kelsey, and I sure as hell am not getting back together with her," he bellowed, stuffing his hands back in his pockets. Otherwise he might've grabbed her by the shoulders and tried to shake some damn sense into her.

She couldn't seriously believe he'd wanted any of this? That he'd orchestrated it?

After everything they'd been through together, didn't she know him better than that? Didn't she know him at all?

Determined to explain himself, he forged ahead like a bull in a china shop. "Kelsey set me up. She tried to kiss me, and I didn't let her. I told her I was with you—that we were happy. That picture? What you saw in the paper? She tripped. The only thing I did for Kelsey was keep her from face planting on the carpet. And believe me, if I could take back those three seconds of chivalry, I sure as hell would've let her bite it."

Chloe pursed her lips. "So you didn't kiss her?"

"No," he said, stepping closer, sensing her resolve melting. "That's what I've been trying to tell you."

"But she tried to kiss you?"

He paused. Where was she going with this?

He had the distinct feeling he was about to step on a landmine, but seeing no other option, he answered truthfully. "Yes. This whole thing is some sick, twisted attempt to, I don't know, salvage our failed relationship. That's why I didn't tell you about it in the first place. I didn't want to hurt you."

Tossing her head back, she laughed that empty, soul-slicing laugh again.

"Are you really such a self-serving jackass? You didn't want to hurt me? So you lied to me instead? Let me find out the truth from Page Six? How's that working out for you, Ryan?" She shook her head, tears filling her eyes. "You know what? Don't answer that. I can't believe I ever trusted you. You can take all your bullshit and shove it up your five hole, Ryan."

"Chloe—"

"You need to leave." Her voice took on that hard edge again and she moved to close the door.

Shit. He kept saying the wrong things, making it worse. Maybe he wasn't explaining it right. There had to be a way to fix it.

"I'm not going anywhere until we figure this out," he said, wedging his toe in the door and holding his ground.

No way was he leaving things like this. Hell, it was worse than he could have imagined.

She'd only just agreed to date him, and now she was ready to turn tail and run? With every fiber of his being he wanted to tell her he loved her, but he wouldn't cheapen the sentiment like that. The first time she heard those words? It wouldn't be him using them as leverage to right a wrong. It would be special, not some last-ditch effort to save their terminal relationship.

He just hoped he'd see that day.

"What is there to figure out?" she asked, her words dangerously low. "You've been manipulating me from the first moment we met. And you know what? I'm done. Done with the manipulation. Done with the lies. Done with this whole fake relationship. You need to leave. Now."

"What are you talking about?" Did she really believe this was all some elaborate ruse? What? That he'd used her to get Kelsey back? To get more press? "You can't really believe that. After all the time we've spent together?"

"Did you take a shot to the head?" she asked, ignoring his questions. She gripped the door so hard her knuckles turned white. "What part of 'leave' don't you understand?"

Quick as a flash, she reached behind the door and grabbed something. His jersey. She flung it at him, hitting him square in the chest. He took a step back, shock rippling through his body.

"Maybe this will clear it up for you. I never want to see your face again."

Clutching the jersey to his chest, with Chloe's scent clinging to the soft fabric, he stood there speechless as she slammed the door and locked it. The sound of the bolt sliding home rang out like a gunshot in the silent hall. He finally understood what it meant to be shot through the heart. And it hurt like a motherfucker.

38

CHLOE

CHLOE PRESSED her back to the door and slid down the cool metal surface. Crumpling to the floor, she pulled her knees to her chest and tucked in her chin. She would not cry over Ryan Douglas. Not again. He'd already gotten too many of her tears and too many sick days.

She was tapped out, both physically and emotionally. Only it seemed her stupid body hadn't gotten the message.

Fresh tears leaked from her eyes, which meant another headache was sure to follow.

Fan-freaking-tastic. Just what she didn't need.

How could she have been so stupid? Letting herself get swept up in the fairytale, thinking maybe she could be enough for a guy like Ryan when she hadn't been enough for Shane the Speedo or, hell, even Dave the Douche.

Happily Never After. That would be her story. It was more apparent than ever.

A sob wrenched from her throat.

Using the sleeve of her sweatshirt, she wiped the tears from her eyes, knowing it was a futile effort. More would spill before the night was through. And why did it have to hurt so freaking bad?

A dozen times before she'd thought her heart was broken, but each of those hurts paled in comparison to what Ryan's betrayal made her feel. She couldn't eat, couldn't sleep, couldn't stop crying. Even her chest hurt, as if she'd been pummeled by love, as if a broken heart were an actual physical ailment. And there was no doubt her heart was broken. Somewhere along the way, she'd fallen for Ryan. Hard. Despite her best efforts to shut him out, he'd slipped past her defenses.

This thing with Ryan? It might have been the real deal if he hadn't gone and fucked the whole thing up. Stupid-controlling-two-timing-good-for-nothing-lying-son-of-a-bitch.

Chloe shuddered. For the first time in her life, telling it like it was made her feel worse, not better. The tightness in her chest refused to subside, and every time she thought of Ryan—in any context—it seemed to get worse. The idea of never seeing Ryan's smiling face again? It was like a penalty shot to the heart.

Without him she felt...empty.

For a brief moment, she wished she'd kept the stupid jersey.

She'd slept in it every night. The damn thing was probably drenched in her tears. Even though his duplicity had shredded her heart, the stupid jersey brought her comfort, reminding her of the good times they'd shared before it had all come crashing down.

Still, she'd meant what she said, she didn't want to see him again. It was too hard.

Tonight's visit had proven it. She'd nearly caved.

The way he'd looked at her with those pleading eyes? One touch and she'd have let him in.

No, she'd just have to learn to live with the pain. Letting Ryan get that close again would be lethal to her resolve.

After all, even if he hadn't kissed Kelsey—and that was a big *if* because she wasn't convinced he hadn't—he'd still lied to her. It didn't matter if it was a lie of omission. He could've told her what happened. Instead he'd hidden it, hoping she'd never find out.

Lies and subterfuge?

That was hardly the foundation for a healthy relationship.

While she'd been blissed out, basking in the glow of the perfect New Year's kiss, he'd been plotting to keep secrets from her. And if he lied about something like this, what else would he lie about? What else had he lied about? He'd been in control since the day they met. She'd refused to acknowledge it, but how many times had he convinced her to do something she didn't want to do? Using her job and her involvement with Garden of Dreams as leverage.

At the time she hadn't thought much of it, but now? In retrospect, she couldn't help but wonder if each of his moves had been calculated. Did she even know him at all? The Blueshirt Challenge, sneaking cookies to the kids, their time at The Garden, Gremlins. Had any of it been real?

Maybe he'd been playing her from the start, feeding her all the right lines to bring her defenses down.

No. She refused to believe it. She knew Ryan better than that.

At least she thought she did. Then again, she never would have believed he was sucking face with Kelsey just moments before kissing her either. It was... It was sick. Twisted. Egotistical.

How could that be the same man who held her close and made love to her like she was the only woman in the world? How could he be so honorable and kind one moment and morph into a complete jackass the next?

Her stomach heaved. It was too much. She was going to throw up.

Covering her mouth, she raced to the bathroom and emptied

the sparse contents of her stomach. Afterward, she stood before the sink, splashing cold water on her cheeks and hating the zombified face that stared back at her.

No two ways about it, she looked like hell.

How long would it take for life to return to normal? For the whole humiliating thing to blow over and for people to move on to the next big scandal? How long could she stomach the internet trolls? They were brutal, but even worse was the pitying stares of her friends and coworkers. They'd gone from looking at her like she'd won the romance lottery to looking worried her brand of shit relationship karma might be contagious.

Worst of all, she was starting to think they were right.

39

RYAN

RYAN STOOD TALL, both hands gripping his stick as Coach screamed at him from the bench. He deserved it. He was having a shitty practice, but try as he might, he couldn't get his head in the game. All he could think about was Chloe and the way she'd looked at him with those big, sad eyes.

Chloe telling him she never wanted to see him again.

Chloe who'd had more than her fair share of heartache.

Chloe who he'd crushed with his arrogance and lies.

It was killing him to know he'd done that to her, that he'd turned out to be exactly the kind of man she hated. To know he'd ruined any chance they had of a future together.

He scanned the ice, taking in his silent teammates.

The line was frustrated with him. It was written all over their faces. Frustration and doubt. Doubt he'd be in any shape to lead them to a win over the Kings, the defending Stanley Cup champs and the same team that had knocked the Rangers out of contention last year. He hated the way his teammate's confidence in him had been shaken, but he couldn't seem to focus.

It was impossible.

It was also the worst fucking timing ever. The team needed the win, but all he could think about was Chloe. The woman had him twisted up in knots. He'd known her all of six weeks and she'd decimated him in a way that Kelsey couldn't even after six years.

With renewed focus, he dropped his stick to the ice, preparing for the play Coach called.

It was a play he'd made a thousand times before. Faceoff, quick pass, breakaway, pass, shoot. His eyes travelled the ice, taking in the positioning of his right and left wing.

Coach blew the whistle and Ryan swept the puck back to Jordy, before taking off down the ice himself. Once he was in position, Jordy would pass the puck back and he'd take the shot. Simple, but effective.

The play was all about speed and precision.

Done right, he'd have no trouble slipping one past the goalie.

Ryan froze. Those weren't his words. They were Chloe's.

Too late he realized he'd missed the pass and completely fucked up the play, once again distracted by thoughts of the woman he loved. The woman who'd broken his heart and shut him out. The puck bounced off the boards and ricocheted into the attack zone as he stared on miserably.

"What the fuck is going on with you today, Douglas?" Coach shouted, throwing his hands up. "Take a walk. Get off my ice and don't come back until your head is in the fucking game!"

Anger sliced through his gut as he stripped off his helmet, his teammates watching his every move. Coach was right. He needed to get it together.

Jordy clapped him on the shoulder as he skated by, making his way to the bench.

The show of solidarity only made him feel worse. He was the team captain for fuck's sake. It was his job to build them up, not drag them down. Problem was, up until that moment, hockey had been his whole life. And it had always been enough. More than enough, really.

Only now it felt empty without Chloe by his side.

He felt empty.

Ryan stormed into the locker room, stopping in front of his locker. He stared at it for a minute, realizing for the first time that maintenance had pounded out the dent he'd made. It didn't seem right. Here he was wrecked, barely able to function, and the stupid locker was good as new, as if that fucking article hadn't ruined everything.

No, that wasn't right. *He'd* ruined everything.

If he'd trusted Chloe with the truth, maybe he wouldn't be in this mess. Kelsey may have set the events in motion, but it had been his choice that had put him in the penalty box. Drawing back his arm, he punched the locker.

The resounding crunch echoed through the locker room.

"Feel better?"

Ryan spun around to find Bash watching him curiously from the door. He glared at his teammate, in no mood for sarcasm.

Bash gestured to his own locker. "By all means, beat the shit out of it if it will help you get your head out of your ass."

"Seriously? Do you really want to do this right now? I'm not in the mood, man."

"You think I give a damn about your mood?" Bash asked, moving to the opposite bench and taking a seat across from Ryan. "Newsflash. It's not all about you." He paused, stripping off his gloves. For the first time, Ryan realized his friend looked tired. Beat, even. Cursing himself, he realized he hadn't even asked how Bask was holding up in light of Kelsey's infidelity. "Or maybe it is. Either way, the team needs you."

He snorted. "Did you see that last play?"

"Dude. Why do you think I'm in here playing Dr. Phil?" Bash

gave him a lopsided grin that didn't quite reach his eyes. "Look, I know you got a lot of personal shit going on right now and it sucks balls, but we need you." He hooked his thumb over his shoulder, motioning toward the ice. "That hack who can't complete a pass or hit the broad side of a barn? Not going to cut it for the Kings. We need a captain who can lead us to first place. We've all worked too hard—you've worked too hard—to let it all go to shit now."

Ryan leaned his head back, resting it against the dented locker.

Bash was right. He owed his team more than heartache and despair. He'd already fucked up with Chloe.

The last thing he wanted to do was screw his team over, too. "How're you holding up?"

"Been better." Bash shrugged and leaned forward, resting his elbows on his knees. Apparently he didn't want to talk about it. Not that Ryan blamed him. Kelsey was the last thing he wanted to talk about with his old friend. "So I take it things with Chloe are... What? On the rocks?"

"More like Judgment Day," he returned, making an apocalyptic gesture with his hands. "She won't talk to me. Won't see me. Wants nothing to do with me. Not that I blame her."

"Jesus-*fucking*-Christ. Since when did you become such a quitter?" Bash shook his head, a sound of disgust on his lips. "The Ryan Douglas I know? He fights for what he wants. Since when has your life ever been easy? You telling me it's all been handed to you? First round draft pick? New York Rangers' Captain? Career ending injury no one thought you'd recover from? Come on, man. That's bullshit, and you know it."

Ryan eyed his friend, frustration pulsing in the pit of his stomach.

He didn't want to hear it. What the hell did Bash know?

Well...maybe more than he'd realized. Bash had been by his

side for years, not just as a Ranger, but even during their college days at University of Minnesota.

Taking his silence as a sign of agreement, Bash continued. "Look, I don't know Chloe, but I know you. If this woman has you turned inside out, she's probably worth fighting for. Women like that don't come along every day."

Wasn't that the truth? It was a lesson Kelsey had taught them both.

One they'd learned the hard way.

"She walked out at the first sign of trouble." Just like Kelsey, he finished silently.

That was the part that stung the most. He'd been so sure Chloe was true, that she'd seen past all the fanfare and fame to the man underneath. In the end, it hadn't been enough though, had it? All it took to send her running was one bullshit article on Page Six.

"I didn't say she was perfect, just that she must be worth the effort," Bash countered. "So she fucked up. Haven't we all? You and I both know this life isn't easy."

"Ain't that the truth," Ryan returned. "Clearly she didn't know what she was getting into."

"Doesn't mean she can't handle it." Bash shrugged and climbed to his feet, stretching his back. "Look, man. Nothing worth having comes easy. You gotta fight for what you want in this life. You taught me that. Just thought you might need a reminder."

Ryan remembered too well.

Bash had struggled with the adjustment to collegiate hockey, and when his parents split up, he'd nearly quit. Eventually, Ryan had talked him into staying. They'd done extra drills together, put in countless hours on the ice, and shared too damn many beers to count. Theirs was a friendship that would weather time, hockey, and the gossip rags. Would he be able to say the same about his relationship with Chloe one day?

Maybe Bash was right. He needed to get his head out of his ass.

He loved Chloe and he'd given up on her—*on them*—too quickly. He'd fucked up by not telling her the truth. If he'd been honest, would she have reacted differently? Given him a chance to explain? Stood by him?

There was only one way to find out. And sitting on his ass feeling sorry for himself wasn't it.

40

─────────

CHLOE

CHLOE TUGGED AT HER COLLAR, cursing the winter wind that cut right through her heavy wool coat. It was cold enough to freeze the balls off a brass monkey, and the forecast was calling for another blizzard. That hadn't stopped her from grabbing drinks with Liv, though. She was done crying over Ryan the Jerk, and the slight buzz from the alcohol would give her a good night's sleep before she returned to work in the morning.

It was time to pull herself together and move on.

She sighed. Easier said than done when there was a New York Ranger sitting on her front stoop for all the world to see. She glanced around, confirming there were no photogs in the vicinity. That was the last thing she needed right now.

Or ever, for that matter.

"Don't worry," Bash said, rising to his feet and stuffing his hands in the pockets of his jeans. "I'm alone. The tabloids are only interested in the exploits of the franchise players. A guy like me really has to get unhinged to make headlines."

What was it with hockey players? Didn't any of them own a coat?

She glanced at her watch. It was getting late. How long had

he been sitting on the freezing cold cement steps? More importantly, she wanted to know what he was up to.

"What are you doing here, Bash?" she asked, temper spiking. No way was she going to feel sorry for him, even if he'd also been on the receiving end of Ryan and Kelsey's shit-tastic New Year's photo spread.

"I just want to talk, if you've got a minute."

Chloe planted her hands on her hips. "Did Ryan send you? Are you doing his dirty work now?"

The guy laughed. A full-on belly laugh. It only pissed her off more.

She was done being the butt of their club jokes.

"You're kidding, right? Ryan would probably kick my ass if he knew we were talking."

"Crisis averted. We aren't talking." She stomped up the stairs, brushing past him without meeting his eyes. "I have nothing to say to you. Or Ryan."

"Have it your way," Bash said as she grabbed the door handle. "I just thought maybe you'd want the whole story."

Chloe cursed under her breath. She'd had all the truth she could handle. Did she really want to hear anything else? She was just starting to feel semi-normal again, piecing her broken heart back together. The last thing she wanted to do was spiral back into the pits of despair.

Unfortunately, curiosity trumped self-preservation.

Her hand fell from the door and she turned back to Bash. "The whole story?"

He nodded, his face somber. "I'm sure you've figured out by now, this is about more than just one picture."

Chloe arched her brow, wondering if she was going to regret her decision to hear him out.

"Ryan told you that Kelsey tried unsuccessfully to seduce him on New Year's Eve?" He looked to her for confirmation. She nodded, not trusting her voice. "I thought you'd want to know he was telling the truth. Kelsey admitted as much when she dumped my ass. She tried to kiss him and he pushed her away. Told her he was with you. That he was happy."

Her shoulders sagged, and for the first time she realized how desperately she'd wanted Ryan's story to be true. Even if they were dunzo.

Bash grinned, but it was a sad smile. "I can only imagine the look on her face when she heard that. I know it's hard to believe, but Kelsey's not a bad person. She had it tough growing up, and it sort of screwed up her priorities in life."

Chloe snorted. She'd walk over hot coals before she'd feel bad for Kelsey the Bitch, a name she'd earned ten times over in Chloe's book.

"Anyway, what you probably don't know is that it all started six years ago at the University of Minnesota. Ryan and I were partying with the hockey team and in walked this wild beauty. She was fun, down to earth, and totally into hockey. Just one of the guys."

"I'll bet," Chloe muttered, rolling her eyes. Didn't take a genius to see where this story was going.

"The three of us became inseparable. We partied, talked sports, got into all kinds of shit. Between the long days and the late nights, I fell in love with Kelsey." He shifted his weight, looking uncomfortable for the first time, his dark eyes cast downward. "Only she had her sights set on Ryan. When he got drafted in the first round, she made her move. We were both too young and dumb to see it at the time, but she played us. Both of us. Strung us along until she figured out who would get the bigger payday. When Ryan got hurt and she started looking at me, I thought maybe the time was right, maybe she would finally love me back. Apparently I was wrong. It was stupid and it nearly cost me my best friend. A fact I have to live with every day."

Well, shit. She hadn't seen that coming.

Despite her best effort to remain detached, her heart broke for him. If anyone could relate to his heartache, she could.

"Ryan never told me that story," she confessed, crossing her arms over her chest, the biting wind forgotten.

"No, he wouldn't." Bash leaned against the railing casually. "He plays it off like it wasn't a big deal, and he clearly didn't care for Kelsey the way he cares for you, but that doesn't mean it didn't leave him bruised and broken. Being used like that? It leaves a guy feeling like maybe his only value is in the game. It's hard to trust when you feel that way."

He'd know, wouldn't he? He'd been through the same thing.

Wait. What did he mean Ryan cared more for her than he'd ever cared for Kelsey? How could he even know that?

"Look, Chloe, I'm sorry you got caught up in all of this, but Ryan is a good guy. It's destroying him to know he's hurt you." He raked a hand through his spikey hair. "In all the time I've known him, I've never seen him like this. He's a mess. His game is a mess. If he doesn't get it straightened out, well, I don't know what Coach will do."

Her gut twisted. Was Ryan's career in jeopardy?

He'd told her once that he feared a trade. But the Rangers were his team. Surely they wouldn't do that to him? He loved the freaking Blueshirts. He'd pushed his body to the limits trying to get back in top shape so he could play for them.

It wasn't fair.

Of course, life was rarely fair. She knew that as well as anyone.

"Anyway," Bash said, straightening to his full height. "I just thought you should know the whole story, not just what they print on Page Six."

"Thanks," she whispered, not sure if she felt empowered or worse for the wear now that she was armed with additional insight into Ryan's actions.

Bash stepped onto the sidewalk and headed west. He took a few steps and turned, as if he'd just remembered something important.

"Of course, anyone who knows Ryan and knows what he's about would never believe the stuff they write in the papers." He tilted his head, studying her. "I have to be honest, I was pulling for you. You're good for Ryan. I've never seen him that happy before, but if one bullshit article in the tabloids is all it takes for you to cut and run, maybe it's best you part ways now because you don't deserve him."

Talk about a sucker punch. Right. To. The. Gut. It was as if all the air had been sucked out of her lungs.

She stood openmouthed as she watched him walk away whistling.

41

CHLOE

CHLOE STARED at the invitation in her hand, feeling a hell of a lot like the cowardly lion. Where was her courage when she needed it most? MIA, apparently. Or maybe hidden at the bottom of a nice bottle of Merlot.

Now there was an idea.

Glancing at the little wine rack on her kitchen counter, she shook her head, casting off the spineless thought. She was a grown ass woman. She had a handle on this.

Didn't she?

Besides, what was the big deal? It was just a peewee hockey game.

A peewee hockey game her ex would be coaching. *Maybe.*

She sighed, knowing that no matter how badly she wanted to skip, she couldn't possibly. The kids from Garden of Dreams had invited her, and she didn't want to let them down. She'd distanced herself from the foundation after her nuclear breakup with Ryan, knowing if she continued her affiliation the odds of running into him at events were pretty good.

Broken heart or not, it had been selfish of her. She

desperately missed the work and the kids. Judging by the invite in her hand, they were missing her, too.

Tonight they'd be playing hockey at The Garden, coached by the Rangers themselves.

Despite the Rangers' involvement, it wasn't exactly billed as standing room only. More likely small and intimate with just the families of the young players and a few select guests in attendance. She was honored to have received an invite. It would be fun—*as long as she could steer clear of Ryan.*

Maybe he wouldn't even be there. How many coaches did they need anyway?

It wasn't like he volunteered at every Rangers event.

And there were twenty-two other players on the team.

Solidifying her resolve, she grabbed her purse and made her way downstairs, where she set out on foot toward the subway. Her belly churned at the thought of facing Ryan. It had been a few weeks since she'd seen him.

Sixteen days and four hours, to be exact. Not that she was counting or anything.

She'd been doing her damnedest to avoid watching his games. Still, it was hard not to hear the snippets of water cooler talk about how he was struggling although the team was moving up in the ranks. The sports blogs were speculating his calf hadn't fully healed, but she knew better.

It wasn't his leg that was the problem. It was his head. Maybe even his heart.

God knew hers was hurting.

When she arrived at the station, she descended the stairs, reaching the platform just in time to catch the N train to Times Square, where she'd hop the red line over to Penn Station.

Unable to stop thinking about what Bash had said, she settled into her seat, wondering for the hundredth time if she'd made a mistake. Was Ryan's career in jeopardy because of her?

Would they trade him at the end of the season? Would he be forced to leave the city? Had her toxic dating history caused her to overreact, ruining the best thing that had ever happened to her?

It wasn't like he'd actually kissed Kelsey.

He hadn't cheated on her or left her or traded her in.

If what Bash said was true, Ryan had actually *chosen* her.

And in his own misguided way, he'd tried to protect her from Kelsey's vindictive actions, just as he'd protected her in the bodega on the night they first met. Because that's who Ryan was. How could she fault him for that? It was one of the many reasons she loved him.

Shit.

She *loved* Ryan Douglas.

The realization hit her like a mob of bargain hunting fashionistas at a sample sale.

Sucking in a deep breath, she tried to ignore the pulse-pounding, hand-shaking wave of panic that crashed through her. There was no denying it. She'd been trying—unsuccessfully—for weeks. She glanced at her watch. Sixteen days and five hours, to be exact. Which was exactly why moving on and putting Ryan in the rearview mirror was proving easier said than done.

Somewhere along the way she'd fallen for him, making the sting of his betrayal that much sharper. Whether he realized it or not, he'd ripped out her heart. The one thing she'd never meant to give him.

The train slid into Times Square, jarring Chloe from her thoughts.

She sighed. There would be plenty of time for self-recrimination later. Climbing to her feet, she made the transfer and arrived at Penn Station with plenty of time to spare.

Squaring her shoulders, she approached the main entrance

of The Garden and presented her invitation for admission. Following the attendant's instructions, she made her way down the empty corridor, her footsteps echoing in the empty space. Déjà vu swept over her as she thought about her private visit to The Garden with Ryan, and her resolve faltered.

She shouldn't have come. She wasn't ready. Not even close.

Turning on her heel, she found herself face to face with Becca.

"You'd better hurry," the other woman said, linking their arms and leading Chloe forward. "The game will be starting soon and the kids were so excited to hear you RSVP'd!"

"Wouldn't miss it for the world." She forced a shaky smile. "Who's coaching the game?"

Becca beamed at her with barely contained enthusiasm. "Wright and Kristiansen are coaching the red team. Skarkowski and Knight have the blue team. And Bischoff and Miller are officiating. It should be lots of fun!"

Disappointment washed over her at the realization Ryan wouldn't be on the ice. Which was silly. An hour ago, she'd been afraid to face him.

Really, it was better this way. The game was about the kids, not her disastrous love life, and the last thing she wanted to do was add drama to their special night.

Following Becca to their seats, she sighed with relief when the other woman chose to sit at the far end of the aisle, near the player's tunnel.

Once everyone was seated, the big screen came to life, introducing the two teams.

Each of the player's profiles were flashed on the screen as they made their way out of the tunnel and onto the ice. Chloe and Becca were on their feet, cheering for the kids and high-fiving the blue team as they passed. They had to stretch to reach the kids down below, but it was worth the effort to see the smiles lighting their faces as they got the official NHL treatment. Chloe noticed some of the parents doing the same at the red team's runway.

The small crowd remained standing through the national anthem and the first faceoff, not taking their seats until the game was well underway. Chloe cheered shamelessly, rooting for both teams. The kids were totally pumped, not that she blamed them. They were getting a once in a lifetime opportunity, playing hockey at The Garden.

She turned to Becca. "Is this a new event? I don't remember seeing it on the roster of last year's activities."

Becca nodded, keeping her eyes fixed on the ice. "Yeah, we just added it."

"It's a great idea," she said, brainstorming ways to promote the event and drive publicity. "Are you planning to repeat it next year?"

"Depends how things go tonight," Becca replied, grinning ear to ear.

Chloe watched as the players skated up and down the ice, noticing for the first time that their jerseys didn't have numbers on the back, but letters. *Odd.* "Hey, what's the deal with the letters on the jerseys?" she asked.

Becca just shrugged, so Chloe returned her attention to the game.

The kids played their little hearts out. It wasn't the hard-hitting game she'd grown to love while watching the Rangers, and their skills could use some work, but their sportsmanship? It was first class all the way. And the coaches were totally invested, calling plays from the bench and heckling the linesmen for bad calls.

For the first time in weeks, Chloe felt like herself. She felt... light. Carefree, even.

When the first period drew to a close, she moved to the

railing, prepared to high-five the blue players again as they retreated to the locker room. What she got instead was a complete surprise.

Isaiah stopped in front of her, stretching up on his toes. "Here you go, Miss Chloe." His eyes shone bright as he handed her a long-stemmed red rose.

"Thank you," she said, unsure what she'd done to deserve the beautiful crimson flower, but flattered nonetheless.

Each blue player did the same, handing her one red rose each until she had collected sixteen of them, creating a fragrant bouquet. The last player off the bench was Janelle. She didn't have a rose, but instead offered Chloe a note before following her teammates down the tunnel.

Dropping into her seat, Chloe cut her eyes at Becca. The other woman just shrugged.

She fingered the small white envelope that had her name scribed on the front. Scanning the crowd, she realized all eyes were on her. None of them looked surprised. Only curious.

Slipping a finger under the seal, she opened the letter, hoping no one would notice how her hands shook.

Chloe,

I'm sorry for being such a colossal jackass. I should have trusted you with the truth. I should have trusted in us. Every day that passes without you by my side feels like an eternity. If you give me the chance, I promise to do things right this time. I will always be on your team.

Ryan

She lowered the note to her lap, studying the roses. It was no coincidence there were sixteen of them. Like her, he'd been counting the days, tortured and miserable.

Sixteen days in hell.

Would it be seventeen? Ryan's message was clear. The puck was in the neutral zone and the next play was hers.

She twisted around in her seat, searching the arena for his familiar face.

It was nowhere to be seen.

Disappointment swept over her once again. *Damn.* She missed him something fierce. Their short time together had changed everything. It had also broken her heart, not something easily forgiven. Or forgotten. And definitely not something she wanted to experience again. But the alternative? That was worse. The idea of never feeling Ryan's lips on hers? Of never lying wrapped in his arms? Her chest tightened. The very idea of it took her breath away.

Sighing, she settled into her seat, waiting for the players to return. Becca patted her hand, a knowing grin on her face.

Although both teams scored in the second period, it felt endless. With thoughts of Ryan distracting her, Chloe was restless. She found herself searching for him constantly, expecting to see him come out of the player's tunnel as he'd done so many times before.

The second period buzzer jarred her from her thoughts. Chloe tensed.

This time, she remained seated as the blue players filed down the runway, unsure of what to expect. Elijah stopped in front of her, hopping up and down on his skates.

"Miss Chloe," he yelled. "Hey, Miss Chloe! I got something for you."

Grinning like a fool, she leaned down to see what Ryan had

in store for her next. Elijah handed her a silver box tied with a gold bow.

"Thank you," she said, giving the package a little shake like she'd seen him do at Christmas. His eyes lit up and he gave her a toothy grin, his dark hair obscuring his eyes.

"Hope you like it," he said, turning and run-walking into the tunnel.

Chloe returned to her seat, sitting with the package on her lap. Unable to suppress the grin on her face, she opened the card.

Chloe,

I'd like to take you on a date. A real date. The kind where I ask and you accept without blackmail. Just you, me, and these shoes. Hope you like them. The way they sparkle reminded me of you.

Ryan

P.S. If you decide to wear nothing but the shoes, I won't complain.

She laughed, a tear leaking from her eye. Another first date? Sounded good to her.

Maybe they could start again after all. A fresh start with no preconceived notions and no ghosts of romances past haunting them. Of course, she wouldn't trade their real first date for some pretentious and formal first date.

In retrospect, it was kind of perfect in its own way. And if he hadn't had the guts to blackmail her? Well, she didn't even want to think about a world in which Ryan hadn't elbowed his way into her life. What was that old saying? You never know what you have until it's gone.

And now that she knew what she'd been missing, she didn't want to go back.

She wanted to move forward.

Pulling the gold bow off the box, she removed the lid to find the most stunning pair of crystal-studded leather and lace Louboutin heels. The shoes were to die for, shining under the bright lights, but what she wanted? What she needed? It didn't come in a box. And it couldn't be bought. She needed Ryan. Needed him like she needed her next damn breath.

She scanned the arena again, desperate to find him waiting for her. No such luck.

What kind of game was he playing?

The third period was even longer than the second, and Chloe was barely able to sit still. She needed to talk to Ryan. To sort out the mess they'd made.

When the game ended on a tie, the players from both teams shared a victory lap around the ice. The audience cheered, rising to their feet. Chloe joined them, watching as the players circled the rink, their cheeks flushed. When they returned to center ice, they lined up. Once all of the players were in position, they turned around, putting their backs to the crowd and revealing the secret of the letters on their jerseys.

Douglas + Jacobs = Power Play

42

RYAN

RYAN CLAMORED DOWN THE STAIRS, taking them two at a time. The cheers of the small crowd masked his thundering approach. When he reached the third row, he stopped, dropping his bag at his feet. Then he stepped up behind Chloe and touched her shoulder.

They were so close he could smell her perfume.

Damn, he'd missed that smell. He'd missed her.

When she spun to face him, there were tears in her eyes. Her lower lip quivered, calling to that archaic side of him that wanted nothing more than to protect her, even if that meant protecting her from his own stupidity. Watching from above as she'd searched the stands for him had nearly been his undoing. He'd wanted nothing more than to rush her side, hold her in his arms, and kiss her senseless.

"What are you doing, Ryan?" She looked around at all the familiar faces surrounding them, uncertainty clouding her eyes. "What is all of this?"

"This is how we court women back in Minnesota. I know this is probably a little old fashioned for a city girl like you, but just humor me, okay? We kind of skipped this part last time." Pulse thundering, he took her hands in his, relieved when she didn't resist. He was ecstatic when she gripped them tight, holding on as if she feared he might disappear in a puff of smoke. "I wanted to do it right this time, so when I ask you to be my girl, there will be no hesitation, no doubt in your mind that you *are* my girl."

Heart damn near beating out of his chest, he withdrew his left hand from hers and reached into the bag at his feet. He pulled out his jersey. It was the same one she'd thrown at him the last time they spoke. He hoped like hell he wasn't about to crash and burn. The soft fabric spilled over their joined hands as he offered it to her.

"I want you to wear my jersey, Chloe. I've missed you like crazy these last couple of weeks and it's been killing me that I hurt you. I fucked up. I know that, but if you give me the chance, I will make it up to you. I'll do whatever it takes to fix this. We make one hell of a team, and we belong together."

She stared into his eyes, just like she had a hundred times before, and for once he really wasn't sure what she was going to say. Would she give him another chance?

Standing before him, she looked so damn beautiful and so unsure of herself. He hated that he'd done that to her, that he'd made her doubt them. Their relationship was the one thing she should always be able to count on, no matter what.

"I..." She sucked in a breath, her shoulders rising and falling. "I screwed up, too. Instead of jumping to conclusions, I should have let you explain. I should have trusted you."

"None of that matters now," he said, tucking her hair behind her ear and cupping her chin. "It's all in the past. There's only one thing I care about right now."

She raised her brow, the corners of her full lips inching upward. "And what's that?"

"I want you to be my girl." He stroked her cheek, relishing the feel of her silky skin. A familiar tension coiled in his gut when he touched her, as if he needed reminding of their explosive chemistry. But that wasn't what this was about. This was about something deeper, something more meaningful than mind-blowing orgasms, although he was thrilled to have those, too. "I need you to be my girl. I love you, Chloe Jacobs."

Staring up at him with wide eyes, she swallowed. Her hands shook as she clutched his jersey to her chest. Was that a good sign? He wasn't certain, but he prayed she wasn't going to fling it back in his face—again.

"You love me?" she whispered.

"I've been trying to figure out how to tell you for weeks," he admitted, shifting his weight. "You don't have to say it back. I just wanted you to know—"

She brought her hand to his lips, silencing him.

Her eyes locked on him as if they were the only two in the quiet arena. "I love you too, Ryan Douglas."

His heart swelled—*fucking swelled*—with joy. He felt like a damn teenager, overwhelmed by the amplified emotions surging through his body. For the first time he realized how nervous he'd been, knowing she might not feel the same way.

Now? There was nothing to fear.

"So what do you say?" he asked, riding the emotional high. "Are you team Douglas-Jacobs?"

There was only a brief moment of hesitation before an ornery grin spread across her face, lighting up her eyes. "I'm more of a Jacobs-Douglas kind of girl."

"Is that right?" He slipped an arm around her waist and pulled her close. Her breath hitched as her body came into contact with his, melting against him as if she'd been made for him alone. "I guess I can live with that."

The laughter that spilled from her lips was music to his ears.

They were going to be okay. Better than okay.

He'd meant what he said. He would do whatever it took to

restore her confidence in him, in them. They'd be stronger than ever and nothing—*nothing*—those fools at Page Six printed was going to tear them apart.

"Shut up and kiss me." She slid her hand around his neck and lowered his mouth to hers. Chloe's lips crashed against his, her tongue darting into his mouth and mating with his own as she held him tight. Now that was something he could get used to.

And this time? He wasn't letting her go.

EPILOGUE

RYAN

RYAN PACED OUTSIDE THE APARTMENT. Gathering his courage, he cursed himself for being such a pussy. What was the big deal? People got engaged every day. Chloe was going to say yes.

Probably.

No, definitely. She wanted this as much as he did.

Maybe she hadn't come right out and said it, or even hinted at it for that matter, but he was sure she'd say yes. And the element of surprise would make it that much sweeter. He couldn't wait to see the look on her face, assuming he didn't butcher the proposal, which was a very real possibility.

Despite hours of practicing, he felt as if a puck were lodged in his throat.

Rolling the tiny box between his fingers, he contemplated the ring inside. He'd chosen a classic princess cut, knowing immediately the simple choice would complement her larger-than-life personality. Plus, he kind of liked the irony of it and he knew she would, too. It would be their private little joke. But there was nothing funny about his intentions. He wanted to spend the rest of his life with her. To build a future together.

The last year had taught him a lot, including the fact that he could live without hockey. He couldn't say the same about Chloe. She would always come first.

Always.

Hell, he should've done it months ago. He loved her with all his heart and soul.

In all his life, he'd never been happier. And with or without hockey, he knew she'd be by his side, supporting him through life's highs and lows. Before Chloe, he hadn't even known what real love was.

Now? He couldn't imagine his life without her in it.

The last couple of months they'd been living together had been amazing. Just having her under his roof had made a world of difference, transforming his sterile apartment into a real home. Their home. It was time to take the next step. *Together.*

Stuffing the ring box in his pocket, he checked his watch.

Still plenty of time to make their reservation uptown. He was ready. He'd practiced the words all day. If he didn't know them by now, he was screw—

What was that smell?

Was that smoke? It sure as hell smelled like it. And it was coming from their apartment.

Scrambling for his keys, he unlocked the door and let himself in. No sooner did he open the door than the smoke alarm started bleating, warning of a potential blaze. Leaving the door open behind him, he ran down the hall, heart pounding erratically.

"Chloe?" He froze when he reached the living space.

Everything looked fine. Normal even, except that the table had been set for two, complete with fresh flowers and flickering candles.

So much for a night on the town.

Maybe he should have called ahead and told Chloe about the reservations.

It had taken him weeks to book a table, and the last thing he wanted to do was give it up, but if she'd cooked dinner, they were definitely staying in.

He sniffed, the acrid scent of smoke irritating his nose. Then again, maybe not. Whatever this was, it was big. Chloe never cooked. *Ever*. It was practically against her religion.

"Chloe? Are you okay?" he called, shouting over the damn alarm. "Where are you?"

A barely audible whimper came from the kitchen. What he heard loud and clear was an unfamiliar *whoosh* and an uncharacteristically PG-rated curse. "Lousy-good-for-nothing-overpriced-food-destroying-piece-of-crap-excuse-for-an-oven!"

Bracing himself for the worst, he squared his shoulders and turned the corner.

Relief flooded his veins. It was impossible to suppress the grin that spread across his face as he took in the scene before him. Chloe stood before the oven in a stained apron, fire extinguisher in hand. He shut off the fire alarm and turned his attention back to his girl, who was staring at what he could only assume was their ruined dinner, coated in a fine white dust.

"Oh, honey, you cooked." He eyed the charred remains and winked at her. "You shouldn't have."

She took one look at him and burst into tears.

CHLOE

BAWLING LIKE A BABY, Chloe collapsed in Ryan's arms, the burned remnants of their romantic dinner taunting her from the stovetop. Ryan scooped her up, circling her body with his warm embrace. All the pressure, all the anxiety slipped away.

She was home, right where she belonged.

"Shhh," he whispered, stroking her hair with one hand and rubbing her back with the other. "I was just teasing. It's no big deal. We'll just go out to eat."

She sniffed, mortified by her impromptu cryfest. Who did that? And why did Ryan have to be so understanding all the time? Especially when she couldn't even prepare one stupid meal without damn near burning the place down. She sighed. There was still a lot to learn about being a domestic goddess.

Or, you know, just being domestic.

"So much for my shit-tastic cooking skills." Pulling away, she grinned up at him, letting him know the worst of her emotional meltdown had passed. "It was worth a shot."

He eyed the blackened oven dubiously. "Princess, what were you thinking?"

It was now or never. Chloe drew a deep breath, calming her deep-fried nerves.

"I thought it would be nice to share a home cooked meal." She pointed at the pans on the stovetop one by one. "Balsamic roasted baby carrots, garlic roasted baby potatoes, and herb roasted baby chicken."

Ryan tilted his head, studying her with curious eyes. "Do I sense a theme to this meal?"

"What?" Chloe asked, stalling for time. *Dammit.* She'd screwed it all up. That hadn't come out right. At. All. "I can't roast shit?"

His eyes sparkled with mischief, and was it her imagination or had his lips quivered as well?

Yep, she'd hit that one right on the head.

"I was referring to all of the baby food."

"Yes, well, about that." She chewed her lower lip, struggling to get the words out. Two little words. Lots of big changes. How would Ryan take it? Would he be excited? Disappointed? Would he feel pressured? Or worse yet, would he bolt? *No.* No more second guessing. She just needed to tell him and let the pucks fall where they may. "I'm...pregnant."

Ryan laughed. The stupid jerk actually laughed.

Here she was about to have an anxiety attack, fearful of his reaction, and he had the audacity to laugh? Not exactly the reaction she'd been expecting. Then again, there were worse reactions to have, right?

Unsure of what to say next, she watched as he dug into his pocket and pulled out a small box. A small box that looked a hell of a lot like a ring box. Was that...?

No. It couldn't be. She shut down the thought immediately.

That was the worst kind of wishful thinking.

"This probably looks bad," Ryan said, shifting his weight and raking his fingers through his hair. "But I was going to surprise you tonight. I made reservations and everything." He flashed her a sheepish grin.

Then, grasping her hands, he fell to one knee.

Chloe's pulse thundered so loudly she could barely form a coherent thought, let alone process what Ryan was saying. He stared up at her with such love, such adoration, his eyes filled to the brim with raw emotion.

"I wanted to do this right. I thought that meant champagne and roses and ambiance. Now I realize doing it right is this right here. *Us.* Together. Happy. In love. Anywhere you go, that's where I need to be. For the rest of my life. Marry me, Chloe. Marry me and make me the luckiest sonofabitch in New York City."

Marry me. Marry me. Marry me.

The phrase echoed through her brain like a song stuck on repeat. And for the first time in her entire life, she was utterly speechless. It was the happiest moment of her life and there were no words to describe it.

Tears leaked from her eyes as she absorbed Ryan's words, knowing they'd be imprinted on her brain until the end of time.

"So what do you say?" he asked, flipping open the tiny box to reveal a fantastic princess cut diamond set in a traditional platinum setting.

The bright kitchen lights set the stone on fire, radiant light bouncing off its flawless surface. It was simple. Elegant. Perfect. It was the most stunning ring she'd ever seen. And it was hers. Forever. Just like Ryan. She could hardly believe it. "Do we have two things to celebrate this evening?"

Chloe nodded, tears running down her cheeks. "Yes," she cried, locking her fingers with Ryan's. "Yes. Yes. *Yes!*"

Climbing to his feet, he pulled her body to his, slipping his hands around her waist and lifting her into the air. He spun them both in a circle like something right out of a fairytale. Only this was no fairytale, it was her life. This was really happening.

She was going to be Ryan's wife and the mother of his child.

It was all so...so...*surreal.*

Heat pooled in her belly, fanning out through her body and warming her limbs.

Without warning, Ryan crushed his lips to hers, peppering her with his soft kisses, each one more tender than the last as he claimed her.

Still reeling from his proposal, Chloe held him tight, unable to believe she, Chloe Jacobs, would soon be Mrs. Ryan Douglas.

It had a nice ring to it.

Holding her gaze, Ryan withdrew his lips.

He pressed a hand to her belly. "I'll bet this little guy is going to be one hell of a hockey player. He'll have quick hands just like his daddy."

Chloe arched her brow. "And what if this little guy is actually a little girl?"

Ryan froze, a look of horror on his face. "A girl?" Apparently he hadn't considered the prospect. He tilted his head. "We're going to need some rules. Rule number one? No dating until she's thirty. Rule number two? No dating hockey players. *Ever.*"

A grin spread over Chloe's face, and she patted his chest. "I think we have some time before we have to worry about the rules of dating."

He kissed her nose. "You're right. We have the rest of our lives to figure it out. Together."

~

Thank you for reading Once Upon a Power Play! Need more Risky Business in your life? Grab Becca's story, Seducing the Fireman!

ALSO BY JENNIFER BONDS

Waverly Wildcats

Holding Harper

Claiming Carter

Catching Quinn

Scoring Sutton

Protecting Piper

The Harts

Miles and Miles of You

Not Today, Cupid

Royally Engaged

A Royal Disaster

Royal Trouble

A Royal Mistake

The Risky Business Series

Once Upon a Dare

Once Upon a Power Play

Seducing the Fireman

ABOUT THE AUTHOR

Jennifer Bonds writes sizzling contemporary romance with sassy heroines, sexy heroes, and a whole lot of mischief. She's a sucker for enemies-to-lovers stories, laugh-out-loud banter, over the top grand gestures, and counts herself lucky to spend her days writing swoonworthy romance thanks to the support of amazing readers like you!

Jen lives in Pennsylvania, where her overactive imagination and weakness for reality TV keep life interesting. She's lucky enough to live with her own real-life hero, two adorable (and sometimes crazy) children, and one rambunctious K9. Loves Buffy, Mexican food, a solid Netflix binge, the Winchester brothers, cupcakes, and all things zombie. Sings off-key.

To connect with Jen, visit www.jenniferbonds.com to sign up for her newsletter and be the first to know about new releases, giveaways, and exclusive content! You can also find her on Facebook, Instagram, and TikTok @jbondswrites.

www.ingramcontent.com/pod-product-compliance
Lightning Source LLC
Chambersburg PA
CBHW061817190726
48289CB00007B/2225